Highland Warrior: Keeper of Secrets

Keeper of Secrets, Volume 1

Elina Emerald

Published by Elina Emerald, 2022.

Copyright

Table of Contents

Dedication

To my family

Prologue

1035 – Folkestone Abbey, Kent, England

"Robert! Robert, *le Magnifique*! My love, where are you? Our son needs you." Duchess Eloise of Normandy was delirious and ranting while on the birthing bed in the abbey.

"Your Grace, all will be well," Abbess Murdina said as she placed a cold compress on Eloise's brow.

"Robert! Why have you abandoned me here? *Abbaye de la Trinité de Fécamp est froide,*" Eloise shouted while reaching out into thin air as if her husband were there.

"What is she saying, Abbess?" Sister Bissett asked.

"She believes she is still at *Fécamp Abbey*. She complains of the cold. It is not a good sign, Sister."

The duchess was perspiring profusely. She clasped Murdina's hand and said, "Has something happened to Robert? What if he dies in the holy land? What will William do to my son?" She collapsed back onto the bed, muttering indecipherable words.

Murdina knew what the duchess spoke of. It was known far and wide that Robert the Duke of Normandy had formally named his illegitimate son William as his heir. It was typical of Robert to refuse to marry his mistresses yet claim his illegitimate children. Except this time, he married Eloise and only a few were privy to it. But Murdina knew because she was present at the wedding in France.

Murdina shook her head at the complication this would cause should the child live.

She did all she could to sooth and calm the duchess while she and Sister Bissett frantically worked throughout the night trying to save both mother and child.

Eloise suddenly clutched Murdina's arm and demanded, "Promise me you will keep him safe until Robert returns?"

"Aye, I promise I will keep your bairn safe."

"It is a boy, I can feel it. We must name him, 'Edmund', that's what Robert wanted. Edmund is a nice name, *oui*?"

"Aye, it is a strong name."

The duchess visibly relaxed, then her body shuddered as if wracked with pain. She bore down, letting out a piercing scream.

Sister Bissett exchanged a worried glance and whispered, "There's too much blood."

Murdina said, "Pray, Sister and dinnae give up."

The sisters worked hard to save the pair, but their efforts were in vain, and the fates unkind. By midnight all was quiet except for the cry of a tiny babe. A babe whose first breath was taken just as his mother breathed her last.

Murdina cradled the tiny baby boy and mourned the loss of his mother.

She whispered, "Welcome to the world, Edmund, tis sorry I am that your life has begun with loss. But we shall make the best of it."

The babe seemed to settle as the abbess soothed him.

Sister Bissett asked, "What happens now? Should we send for the duke?"

Murdina replied, "Robert is dead. He perished on the journey back from Jerusalem, just outside of Nicaea. William is the Duke of Normandy now. I did not have the heart to tell the duchess. The missive arrived this morning."

"Oh Abbess, what a tragedy," Sister Bissett said as she made the sign of the cross.

"Arrange a proper burial and notify her family."

"And what of the bairn?"

This abbey is a denizen of *Normandy*. We will take him with us. I will send a missive to Brother Mateo for his assistance. Send a message to the *Order*, the child will need parents."

"Aye, it shall be done. Did the duke make any provisions for his family?"

"He did. A parcel of land, some coin and an annuity for the duchess should he pass before her. It will be held in trust until Edmund reaches majority."

"That is more than most noblemen leave their families."

"Aye, but Robert was not your ordinary nobleman. He was kind."

"Did you ken the late duke, Abbess Murdina?"

"A long time ago. A very long time ago."

"Then I am sorry for your loss as well."

Murdina just nodded, then said, "Oh, and one more thing, Sister Bissett."

"Aye."

"Whatever happens, William must never ken he has a legitimate half-brother."

Chapter 1

1036 - Saddell Abbey, Argyll, Scotland

"Please dinnae leave me here, Papa, please. I promise to be good. I will not eat much, and I'll stay out of sight." Yesenda clung to her father. Her arms wound tight around his waist, her cheek resting against his stomach.

Grant MacDonald was a large imposing figure who rarely showed emotion unless it came to his twelve-year-old daughter. His features softened as he held her tight and tried to placate her.

"Och, come now sweeting. Tis not a punishment leaving you at the abbey, tis a blessing. You will learn much more from the sisters than me, and my war band can teach you."

"No, I only want to learn from you, Papa. You can teach me anything," she said, sobbing.

He gently stroked the back of her hair as he whispered and gentled his voice, "With your *màthair* gone, you need a woman's touch and a fine education. I cannot teach you those things, sweeting. This is the best place for you."

"I dinnae need women. Please, Da, I can learn everything from you."

"*Mo nighean*, you are a lass, and you need to learn womanly things."

Yesenda began sobbing in earnest. She could not bear to be separated from all she held dear; it was too much for her pre-teen emotions to process.

"But I dinnae need those things, Papa. I want to be a warrior. I will learn more from your men than what nuns can teach me." Yesenda had worked herself into a state.

Grant softly smiled, then he crouched down so he could speak to her properly.

"Yesenda, someday you will make a fine warrior. But you need women to teach you how to become a fine mistress for the clan. Now, dinnae embarrass our clan with this watery display." He smiled to soften the reproach.

Yesenda sniffed, then remembered they had an audience. A nun and two novices stood a short distance away. Her spine straightened. Yesenda wiped her tears and said, "Sorry Papa, tis just that I... I... love you and I will miss you." She hiccupped the words.

His eyes softened and glistened with unshed tears. It was the only outward sign that it was difficult for him to part with her, too. "I love you, sweeting. More than anything in the world. It's why I need to do this. I'll visit as soon as I can." His voice cracked slightly, then he cleared his throat and said, "Come now, the sisters are waiting. MacDonald's dinnae keep people waiting."

With those words, he hugged Yesenda once more, wiped the tears from her eyes and kissed her cheek, then stepped away and ushered her towards the women. When Yesenda was standing beside the nuns, her father smiled at her one last time, then took his leave. Yesenda watched him slowly disappear down the cloister, his gait sure and strong. He turned back once, waved, and she frantically waved in return. Then he was gone.

That was the last time Yesenda saw her father alive. Because a month later, Laird MacDonald was killed in a skirmish with a hostile clan. When news reached the abbey, Yesenda was inconsolable that she would never see her beloved father again. She had lost both parents within a year, and she was far from home, where her heart ached to return.

Yesenda's older brother, Ruadh took over as laird and she wrote several times begging Ruadh to let her return home, but each time he replied telling her it was not safe. Still, she begged until finally she gave up.

Yesenda vowed never to love anyone again because everyone she loved either died or abandoned her.

The Refectory, Saddell Abbey

IT HAD BEEN SEVERAL weeks since her father passed and Yesenda kept to herself. She did not converse or engage other than was necessary to show politeness. The combination of grief and homesickness was debilitating some days. Another reason she kept to herself was a handful of girls tormented and bullied all newcomers, and especially the most vulnerable. The tormentors came from wealthy families and the ringleaders were Eilidh Ruthven and Una Pringle. Whilst Yesenda could understand that some people were just mean, she could not excuse the fact Sister Ines, who supervised the common assemblies, turned a blind eye to it.

So Yesenda did everything in her power to remain invisible. To not attract any unwarranted attention. It was safer that way. Each night before going to bed, she prayed for deliverance from the abbey and from the strange new world she now occupied.

While the girls tormented everyone on a whim, they seemed more vicious towards one newcomer called Naomi. She was Italian, and Yesenda noted they were almost the opposite in physical appearance. Yesenda was blonde-haired and fair. She wore her long locks loose and her build was leaner, taller. Naomi's skin tone was sun kissed bronze, and her hair was a lustrous black. She wore it in two long braids. Naomi was shorter and curvaceous but there was a sadness in Naomi's dark brown eyes that Yesenda felt an affinity with.

Whenever she saw Naomi, it was like she was peering into a mirror, reflecting her own debilitating grief and homesickness. Under any other circumstances, Yesenda would have loved to talk to her, but to be anywhere around Naomi meant attracting the vitriol of the terrible two, so she kept her distance and remained invisible.

One day, Yesenda was in the refectory quietly tucked away in a corner, eating her meal. She kept her head down. When the trouble began.

She heard a commotion and quickly glanced up just in time to watch Una push Naomi. The latter fell to her knees, dropping her plate of food onto the floor. Naomi kept her head down and quickly tried to clean up the mess.

Yesenda's eyes scanned the room, and she noticed the other girls watching quietly but trying to avert their eyes. Meanwhile, Sister Ines smirked and pretended to be occupied with something else.

"Naomi, you dinnae belong here. No one likes you, foreigner," Eilidh said, now moving closer. She surreptitiously tipped over Naomi's dish with the tip of her shoe again, spilling the contents Naomi had just picked up.

Naomi remained still and did not move. Her head lowered in submission.

"You're so clumsy, always falling over making a mess," Una said as she kicked Naomi in the spine. Naomi made a subtle grunt and tried to move out of their way, but Eilidh stood on the end of her long braid so she could not move far without it hurting her scalp.

Yesenda gripped her spoon tighter, watching the display, willing it to be over soon.

Dinnae get involved, she chanted in her head over and over. They would soon tire of it and move on as they had times before. Except this time, something changed. Their treatment was worse.

Naomi tried again to pick up her dish when Una placed her foot on Naomi's hand. Effectively crushing her fingers. Naomi winced but did not make a sound.

It was when Naomi looked up and stared straight at Yesenda that she saw her expression. It was filled with pain. Naomi was biting her lip to keep from crying out, and that sadness as bleak as Yesenda's own stared back at her. Yesenda saw something else in Naomi's eyes. *Hopelessness.*

Without hesitation, Yesenda rose from her chair and yelled, "Leave her alone!"

The refectory grew quiet. There was a brief pause before everyone stared at Yesenda including Una and Eilidh. Yesenda realized it was too late to back down now.

The two girls eyed her up and down, then snorted. Una ground her foot harder into Naomi's hand, almost taunting Yesenda to do something.

And she did. As if borne of instinct, Yesenda picked up the uneaten apple on her plate and threw it will all her might at Una's head. By some stroke of luck, her aim was true, and it smacked the girl right in the forehead with a loud *'thwacking'* sound.

Una staggered backwards with a grunt, and Eilidh stepped away from Naomi in shock. Naomi looked stunned, but quickly grabbed her plate and scurried out of the way.

Yesenda plucked an apple off the girl's plate beside her and this time took aim at Eilidh. Again, her aim was perfect, and Eilidh screeched, "Sister Ines! Yesenda is attacking us."

Before Yesenda could do anything else, someone gripped her arm and forcibly yanked her away from the table.

"What is the meaning of such violence?" Sister Ines shouted whilst painfully clutching Yesenda's arm. Her nails digging into her skin. As if Yesenda was the one in the wrong.

Yesenda watched as the refectory went silent with wide eyes. Meanwhile, the two perpetrators were behaving as if they were the victims. Caterwauling like toddlers.

Sister Ines shoved Yesenda to stand in the middle of the room. She said, "Violence tis the work of the devil. You think to bring your vile nature here and sully this peaceful place. How dare you!"

Yesenda looked at the sister and felt indignation. Seeing as she had already shattered her cloak of invisibility, she decided she had nothing to lose, so Yesenda loosened her tongue.

"Dinnae talk to me about violence when you allow those vile creatures to torment us all. The devil is the ultimate deceiver, and they continue to lie and yet you, Sister Ines, allow it. How. Dare. You!"

Sister Ines stared at Yesenda in shock before backhanding her hard across the face. "Insolent child!" she shouted and raised her arm to slap her again. Yesenda braced but never felt the slap because a woman dressed in travel clothes suddenly appeared beside Sister Ines and gripped her arm.

"Sister Ines, we dinnae manhandle our charges. Go to the chapel and reflect upon your actions this day," she commanded.

Sister Ines huffed and gave Yesenda a dirty look, then stormed out of the refectory.

The woman then addressed the room. "Now, will someone tell me what on earth is going on here?"

Una stepped forward and said, "Abbess Murdina, Naomi has been stealing food from the scullery and we tried to stop her, but Yesenda threw apples at us."

"*Bugiarda!* I do not steal food. They pushed me for no reason," Naomi yelled from her spot in the corner.

"And what of your part in this?" Murdina asked Yesenda.

"Tis true I hit them with apples, and I am not sorry for it."

"Why did you feel the need to hurl fruit about the room?"

"They were hurting Naomi for their own pleasure. I wanted them to stop."

"You are lying," Eilidh shouted.

"Tis your word against theirs. Unless there is anyone else willing to give their version of events?" Murdina looked about the room.

There was no answer, and the girls lowered their eyes to the floor.

Then Abbess Murdina said, "Very well. I will have to dig deeper. Sister Bissett?" Murdina called behind her.

Another sister entered the room, also in travel clothes. "Aye, Mother Abbess."

Take these four outside please and I will ask the assembly which version is the truth.

It was the first time Una and Eilidh paled.

Ten minutes later, the abbess emerged from the refectory with a stormy expression and said, "Una and Eilidh, you will come with me now! Yesenda, go finish your meal and please refrain from throwing fruit."

Yesenda nodded, relieved she would not get into any more trouble.

Abbess Murdina's expression softened when she addressed Naomi. She said, "Lass, the cook has made up a fresh plate for you."

Naomi said, "Thank you, Mother Abbess."

Naomi and Yesenda slowly walked back into the refectory. The tension had lifted. Yesenda felt all eyes on her, except this time it felt different. Each girl nodded to her as she passed them. It was a silent acknowledgement that the balance of power shifted that day. Without coercion or fear, the other girls told the truth.

Instead of going to her own seat, Naomi brought her food over and sat beside Yesenda. As they settled side by side, it seemed for the first time in a long while, everything was right with the world.

"Thank you for speaking up for me," Naomi said.

"Tis all right. I am sorry I did not do it sooner," Yesenda replied.

"Una and Eilidh will be furious. I urge you to be on your guard at night, for that is when they strike."

"Aye, I will keep that in mind."

Naomi smiled and Yesenda returned it, then they enjoyed their meal together.

They say the strongest bonds are forged in fire. That day, Yesenda and Naomi created a powerful bond that would serve them well in the years to come.

Chapter 2

Fight to the Death

Several nights later Yesenda had just drifted off to sleep in her cell when her nightmare began.

"Get up!" someone said in the dark.

Yesenda felt a splash of cold water on her face. A hand clasped over her mouth, and she was unceremoniously dragged from the bed by her hair. She hit the floor with a hard thump. Yesenda groaned at the shooting pain along her hip when she slammed onto the cold stone floor. She tried to rise but a foot pressed down on her chest to keep her down. She could not see her attackers clearly, but she heard the whispered giggles, and she knew it was them. Her tormentors, Una and Eilidh seeking vengeance for her interference.

Una said, "After your show of bravery in the refectory, we need to teach the other girls that no one crosses us without paying dearly for it. Now that your father is dead, that makes you a worthless bitch like the foreign slut you tried to help."

Yesenda tried to move, but she could not with the weight confining her chest. She felt around for her stick that she kept near the bed but could not reach it. In the dark, she could just make out their shadowy figures and clearly, they meant to frighten her.

What they failed to realize was Yesenda had spent most of her time in the company of her father and his warriors. She had learned a thing or two about fighting and she would die before she lay helpless on the ground.

They had pinned her chest down, but her legs were free. That was their first mistake. Yesenda twisted her hip and with as much strength as she could muster; she raised her leg and kicked Una behind the knee. The girl toppled over, losing balance and hit the wooden frame of the bed hard.

With the foot off her chest, Yesenda could breathe easier, and she twisted her hip to the opposite side and kicked Eilidh straight in the face. She heard an *'oomph'* sound as the sole of her foot connected with flesh. Then Yesenda scrambled to her feet and pushed Una out of the way. Una grabbed Yesenda by the neck and did a choke hold, pulling her back down to the floor.

Yesenda did a grapple move and rolled them, so she was straddling Una and keeping her pinned to the floor. Whether it was the shock of being attacked at night, or the months of pent-up frustration and grief, Yesenda was not sure, but she unleashed all her fury with her fists.

Una screamed in pain, yelling, "Get her off me!"

Eilidh tried to come to her rescue and pulled Yesenda's hair so hard Yesenda felt the burning in her scalp. That was all it took. Something snapped in Yesenda that night and suddenly she did not care if she lived or died. All she cared about was beating the two girls to a pulp.

Yesenda reached behind her, grabbed Eilidh's face and dug her nails into her cheeks, drawing blood. Eilidh released her grip on Yesenda's hair and cried out in pain, frantically trying to pry Yesenda's fingers from her face. Yesenda pulled her down until she, too, was on the floor next to Una, then she lashed out in the dark with her fists. Yesenda heard their shouts of pain as her fists wreaked havoc. Then she heard their panicked conversation.

"Let's go, let's go before sister Bissett finds us."

There was panic and desperation in their voices. Eventually Una got free and tried to pull Eilidh out of the room. But not done yet, Yesenda reached out, yanking one escapee back and punched her in the nose. Then she felt Una try to scramble past her. Yesenda lunged forward, grabbed Una's leg, and bit down hard into the flesh. Una screamed in pain.

All the while, Yesenda fought like a wildcat. She used every inch of her body to lash out at her two tormenters.

Before long, footsteps were heard running down the hallway. The door burst open, admitting light into the room. Yesenda rolled and grabbed her stick on the other side of the bed and held it out in front of her, ready to take on whoever else was coming through that door. She had a feral look on her face, like she was ready to fight to the death.

However, it was not more attackers but someone else entirely. The light illuminated her face and caught the burnished tint of her hair.

"What is the meaning of this?" Abbess Murdina demanded.

"She tried to attack us," Una said.

Yesenda closed her eyes momentarily, knowing she would most likely be punished now for fighting. She lowered her head and stared at the floor. Then lifted her eyes when the abbess asked, "Then why are you both in her room? Did Yesenda call you both in here so she could attack you in the middle of the night?"

They tried to answer but came up empty.

"Yesenda, what happened?" the abbess asked.

Yesenda kept panting as she stared at the girls. She noticed both looked terrible. They had cuts and abrasions to the face and neck, and both were sporting swollen eyes.

Then she said, "They came into my room uninvited. I wanted to make it clear they were not welcome."

Yesenda saw a flash of amusement cross the abbess's face before she hid it.

The abbess cleared her throat and said, "My patience is done with you two, Una and Eilidh. You can be sure I will send a missive to your parents in the morn. In the meantime, there will be no more moving about rooms at night. Go back to your beds now."

"But Abbess Murdina, twas Yesenda's fault —"

"I said leave now or so help me. I'll throw you both out into the street right now. Do you hear me?" Her voice was laced with steel.

They gasped, then quickly scrambled away.

When they had gone, the abbess stood for a moment and stared at Yesenda as if she found something amusing. Then she tsked and said, "Good lord child, you scared the devil out of those two. You ken violence is not the answer to everything?"

"They started it—"

"Aye, I ken it," Abbess Murdina said, raising her hand palm up. "Calm down, you dinnae need to explain what happened. They're fortunate you did not maim them."

Yesenda still hadn't moved or relaxed her position.

The abbess sighed then said, "Lass, the way you hold that thing is all wrong."

She took the stick off Yesenda, repositioned her wrists at a different angle, then placed the stick back in her hands.

"Two hands, Yesenda, and your back foot a few paces behind. That allows you to pivot without losing your balance."

Abbess Murdina gently nudged Yesenda's foot to alter her current stance. "You must stay fluid and always remain on your feet. Like this."

The abbess then pulled a short staff from the sleeve of her gown. To Yesenda's surprise, it extended. Then, without warning, she swiped it at Yesenda. Yesenda immediately pivoted. She lifted her stick and blocked the hit.

The abbess grinned and said, "Well done, lass. You, see? When your stance is right, you have better control from the core of your body." She gestured toward Yesenda's stomach and hips. "And always keep a weapon nearby when you sleep. One must always be prepared for an attack."

Yesenda nodded, still slightly reeling at the bizarre conversation she was having with the abbess.

The abbess then sat on the bed and said, "I have heard from some of the other girls about Una and Eilidh. It was remiss of me to not ken what was going on sooner and leave Sister Ines to watch over them. But I assure you, I will keep a keener eye over my charges."

"Thank you, Abbess."

"Now, I will send sister Bissett in here to tend to your wounds. In the meantime, get some rest."

Murdina rose and walked towards the door. Then she paused and said, "I asked several girls what happened in the refectory that day. They said you protected Naomi. Why did you? You dinnae ken Naomi well, and you usually keep to yourself."

Yesenda took a deep breath and said, "I... I ken what it is like to feel alone in the world. I did not want her to feel she had to face them alone."

The abbess smiled. "Aye, tis a brave thing you did, lass. To make a stand when the safer option would be to remain quiet and do nothing." Murdina paused as if contemplating something, then said, "How would you like to learn to defend yourself so there is never a need to attack?"

Yesenda looked surprised. "I would like that very much if you will teach me."

"I will. But you must keep up with your studies and attend vespers."

Yesenda nodded. "Aye, I can do that."

"Then it is done. Tomorrow, I will introduce you to a... different lesson plan."

"Abbess, may I ask a favor?"

"Aye."

"Can Naomi train too? I fear she desperately needs to ken how to protect herself."

The abbess grinned again and said, "Dinnae worry, I visited Naomi earlier. It would seem you have more in common than you both ken."

"Thank you."

"Oh, and one more thing, Yesenda. I need you to choose a name."

"A name?"

"Aye. Once you agree to work with me, I require my pupils to use a different name when we are not within the abbey walls. So, choose a name."

Yesenda pondered it a while, then said, "Miriam Ferguson."

"Why did you choose that name?"

"Miriam was my mother's name, and Ferguson was my grandmother's clan. I was close to them both."

"It is a fine name. By the way, how good are you at keeping secrets?"

"I have no one to tell."

"Then you'll do Miriam Ferguson, you'll do."

The Order

SEVERAL DAYS LATER, Murdina spoke to an old friend. He was an Italian monk from *Montecassino Abbey* in the mountains of *Lasio*.

"Brother Mateo, I have taken on two new pupils. I would like you to have a hand in their training."

"Se sono adatti," he said and shrugged.

"Aye, I think they are very suitable. One of them is a laird's daughter. The other hails from your homeland, *Castelnuovo dell'Abatei* in *Tuscany*. Her parents worked at the *Abbey of Sant'Antimo*.

Brother Mateo nodded his head while listening, then said, "We shall see."

ABBESS MURDINA SUMMONED Yesenda and Naomi to meet in a large room used for activities. When they arrived, the abbess stood next to a monk Yesenda had never seen before.

"Badessa Murdina speaks highly of you both," he said. "I am Brother Mateo. I would like to test your skills if I may?"

Naomi shrugged her shoulders. Yesenda remained silent.

"You." He pointed at Yesenda. "Show me what you know." Brother Mateo tossed a wooden quarterstaff at her.

He walked over to a pitcher with wine. Poured himself a cup and held it in his right hand. Then he picked up a normal stick with his left hand and said, "Use your weapon to make me spill the wine in this cup."

Yesenda ran at him and did a spin through with the staff aiming for the cup.

Mateo waited, then sidestepped and blocked her staff with his stick. He spun the stick and whacked her hip.

"Ouch!" she said. "You didna say you would hit me back."

Brother Mateo said, "First lesson. The enemy comes with no warning. Again!"

Yesenda ran at him again, this time aiming her staff with more precision. She attempted to hit his elbow. Brother Mateo dodged the hit and whacked the back of her leg. Yesenda noted his movements were fast and fluid. No wine spilled from the cup.

She tried again and missed. Then she felt a hit to her shoulder blade.

"*Prova di nuovo,*" he said.

Yesenda looked confused.

"It means try again."

Yesenda tried to trick him this time. She jerked the staff forward, then tossed it to her other hand and swiped at the cup. It connected and, for a suspended moment in time; the cup tilted forward, threatening to spill its contents. Yesenda held her breath, expecting victory, but Mateo used his stick to catch the cup and tilt it back upright. The base of the cup was now balanced on his stick.

Yesenda's mouth dropped wide open at the move. Mateo grabbed the cup and whacked her arm.

"Ouch!" Yesenda became angry and ran at him. Again, he dodged at the last minute and moved out of the way. She fell face first, panting for breath.

She came at him again and he kicked her legs out from under her. She hit the floor hard.

"Alzarsi!" he demanded.

Yesenda furrowed her brow.

"It means get up," Naomi said.

Yesenda groaned and got up.

"Controlla la tua rabbia!" Brother Mateo said.

"What does that even mean?" Yesenda huffed in frustration.

Mateo said, "It means control your anger. Never allow emotions to rule your head. It is the fastest way to die."

Yesenda sobered at his words. He was right. She had spent more time getting hit with his stick than anything else. She was so grateful when he called for Naomi to take her turn.

No matter how hard Naomi tried, she too could not spill an ounce of wine.

After a tiring afternoon where both girls spent more time sprawled on the floor, Brother Mateo gave his verdict.

He rubbed his chin, paced a little, then nodded and said, "I will train you both."

"Well done, lassies. Now, the actual work begins," Murdina said.

FIVE YEARS LATER, WHEN Yesenda turned seventeen, Brother Mateo introduced her to an unfamiliar weapon. It had a long handle, but the head was made of bronze and contained eight spiked flanges. He called it a mace. It was heavier than the quarterstaff she was used to, but the rudimentary movement patterns she used for the staff were similar. Yesenda just had to adjust the spin to incorporate the extra weight. That was the same year Naomi and Yesenda officially became members of the *Ordine Secretorum*. A secret order of women trained in combat with the purpose of protecting the vulnerable.

They gifted Yesenda a mace forged in Italy, including a black robe with an insignia in the inlay. It was a mace crossed over an iron quarterstaff.

"Do you vow to keep our secrets, protect the vulnerable and serve the order when called upon?" the abbess asked.

Yesenda replied, "I do."

"Welcome to the Order, Miriam Ferguson."

Chapter 3

1043 – Iain's Cottage, Henderson Land, Glencoe

"**W**hy can you not be more ambitious?" Liosa Haxton pouted and paced the room. "Cruim is a weak, pitiful man. You could easily challenge him for the lairdship."

"Liosa, I've told you before, tis not wise to challenge Cruim when he still holds so much power. Besides, Bram is the one who should lead because—"

"Iain Henderson! Why should your cousin be the next laird? You are as good, if not better, than him. You should claim the lairdship for yourself."

Iain sighed. "Liosa, I dinnae want to be laird, and the clan respects and follows Bram because regardless of what you think, he is a born leader. When he becomes the next Henderson laird, I will pledge my fealty to him. We are not just cousins, he is like a brother to me. His family is my family."

"Iain, you will never become anything more than a warrior or farmer if you dinnae aspire to anything beyond this place. Dinnae, you want more from your life?"

"No, Liosa, I am happy to serve my clan and my kin. They are your clan too, you ken. This land, this soil, it's in our blood."

She snorted.

Iain had to contend with similar arguments on a weekly basis. He loved Liosa from the first moment he saw her, when they were just children. But nowadays, all she did was complain. Nothing he did was ever enough. Still, he tried to please her.

Eventually he gave in and challenged Cruim for the lairdship. It ended in disaster with Iain lying in Bram's house with broken ribs, an infected stab wound to his thigh, and a body covered from head to toe in bruises. It was Bram and his brother, Niall, who intervened on Iain's behalf and saved him from certain death.

It was his cousin Willa, his aunt Fia and his sister Tyra who tended his wounds day and night, ensuring he survived the fever that had set in.

"Honestly, brother, you have so little sense listening to that woman," Bram said.

Iain was in too much pain to respond, but asked, "Where is Liosa? Please send her to me."

"Liosa is gone! She was here long enough to show her disappointment that you lost the challenge and she left," his sister Tyra growled.

"No, she has had a trying day. She probably doesna want to see me like this."

"Cousin, dinnae delude yourself. That woman has left you high and dry and you deserve so much better," Bram said.

"Wheesht, Bram! I am going to marry Liosa. She will be my wife and the mother of my bairns."

The room fell silent after Iain made that statement. His aunt Fia just shook her head in disappointment.

"You're a damn fool, brother," Tyra said before she stormed out of the cottage.

When Liosa eventually returned, Iain proposed three times and each time she refused, yet she insisted they remain lovers.

Iain patiently waited for her to change her mind. It never happened. She was eager to bed him when she saw him, then she would disappear for weeks while he waited in hope.

Five long years passed in this manner. As the seasons changed, he waited and with each new year, a tiny part of that hope diminished.

1047 - The Battle of Val-ès-Dunes, Caen, Normandy

WILLIAM THE DUKE OF Normandy had gone by several names in his brief life. William the Bastard being the most prominent, but he aspired to become a conqueror and king of England. He had a thirst for power and ever since he came into his minority; he knew he was destined for great things, and nothing would stand in his way.

William inherited a dukedom with the backing of King Henry of France and even though he was the illegitimate son of Robert, Duke of Normandy, and his mistress Herleva of *Falaise,* Robert named William his heir.

William loved his parents, and it was a blow when his father died. William had a paternal half-sister, Adeliza, and maternal half-brothers, Odo and Robert. He was close to all his siblings and, with his rise to prominence, he ensured they were taken care of as well. By the same token, he knew gaining a position was the simple part, maintaining power was the real challenge.

Which is why William was currently knee deep in mud coming off the battlefield drenched in perspiration and covered in blood.

He walked into his tent as his man helped removed his armor and battle gear. William was reeling at the audacity of his cousin Guy of Brionne and the barons he sided with to oust William as duke.

His brother Odo sat quietly on a bench, trying to read William's mood.

"You did well, brother," Odo said.

"Barely. Curse my damn cousin and his moronic attempt to gain power. If it was not for King Henry's support, I would have perished and Normandy would be lost to me, to us both, brother."

William walked towards the pitcher of water. He washed the blood off his face and hands. The battle was fierce and had resorted to a battle of cavalry. His battle horse had served him well this day.

"Thank God they were a disorganized bunch of rebels. I trampled more of them with my trusty steed as they retreated, and a lot more drowned in the Orne."

"You did well. You stand victorious and this reaffirms to others that you do not take direct threats lightly."

William nodded at Odo. They were close and Odo always offered wise council.

"You know you could have helped me?" William said.

"*Oui*. But as I am the Bishop Earl now, it is not good to appear on a battlefield. You know that thing about being peaceful and not taking up weapons?"

William just snorted. Odo was the bloodthirsty one in their family. He had no qualms caving in someone's head with a club, as long as no one saw it.

"I wonder why your cousin thought he had a better claim to the dukedom than you?" Odo asked.

William said, "Guy mentioned father had a legitimate heir. I sent a spy into his camp, and my man said the same thing."

Odo sat up and straightened. "What exactly did your spy say?"

"Just that there was a male born to a French woman. Father supposedly married her before he went on pilgrimage. He must have loved her a great deal to marry her," William said.

"Please, your father is not capable of love. Remember, he gave our mother Herleva to my father so he could provide for her. This after swearing his undying love for her."

"You have it wrong, brother. He loved our mother, but a duke cannot marry a tanner's daughter, so the next best thing he could do to provide for her and ensure she would not become a pariah was to marry her off to his nobleman."

"Perhaps you a right, William. But he has already named you his heir. It is not good form to then sire a legitimate son to replace you."

"That's why I said he must have loved her a great deal, whoever she is. How would we find this child?" William asked.

Odo replied, "If he is legitimate, then the first place to begin is with the church. There should be records and a paper trail at least. Then we can work from there."

William nodded. "Then it is a good thing you are a bishop. I charge you with finding my dear baby brother."

Falaise Castle, Normandy, France - Several Months Later

"WILLIAM, WE HAVE A problem."

"What is it, Odo?"

"It's true. Your father Robert married, and a legitimate male heir was borne out of the union. This child has a stronger claim to the dukedom. If one of the Barons were to decide to take this child under their wing, they could oust you and act as regent until he attains majority."

"Where are the woman and child?"

"The woman died in childbirth. The whereabouts of the child is uncertain. But my sources believe they sent the babe to an abbey somewhere in Scotland. My men have been searching for him."

"Have they discovered anything else?"

"*Oui,* the name of a woman who is duty bound to protect the boy."

"What is her name?"

"Miriam Ferguson."

"Find them and bring them to me."

Chapter 4

1048 – Saddell Abbey, Scotland

"You wanted to see me, Abbess Murdina?"

"Aye, there is some news I must impart to you."

Yesenda gave her a querying look. "And what of this news?"

"Your brother Laird Ruadh MacDonald sent a missive asking that I prepare you."

"Prepare me for what?" Yesenda asked. She braced herself.

"Laird Ruadh and his men are on their way here to take you... home."

Yesenda stared at the wall for several moments, utterly speechless, then she asked, "But why? He has kept me sequestered here for fifteen years. I dinnae understand. Unless he means for me to act as chatelaine at the Keep?"

She glanced at the abbess, who slightly grimaced.

Then it dawned on her. Yesenda stood and started pacing the room. "No!" He cannot mean to marry me off to some stranger, does he?" She stopped pacing, turned and looked directly at the abbess.

The expression on the abbess's face confirmed her fears.

"Absolutely not! I refuse to be bartered over some land or such nuisance. I cannot believe it!" Yesenda began pacing again. "He abandons me, then expects to pull me out without a moment's notice. Please Abbess Murdina, you cannot let this happen."

"I am afraid I have no choice. He is your guardian, and until you are wed, you are under his protection. Tis why I wanted to speak to you myself. I think this is an excellent decision."

Yesenda looked as if she had been hit. "What? Why? I love it here. I dinnae want to leave now. There is too much on the line."

"Calm down. You need to go, Yesenda. Tis time you left the abbey and went further afield. You are four and twenty now."

"But I cannot. My duty is to the Order she whispered."

"And your duty does not end the moment you walk out those doors."

"What do you mean?"

"This situation is in our best interests."

"How so?"

"Sit down and let us speak calmly. Put aside your emotions and listen to reason."

Yesenda sat and tried not to fidget. She was still reeling from the news.

The abbess poured her a calming brew and then sat down across from her.

"Men have been searching for Edmund. I think your talents are best served outside of the abbey than within it. Our reach from here is limited. Out there, you have the freedom of movement without eyes upon you."

"What has happened?"

"More than we bargained for, I'm afraid. I need you to guard them and keep watch until it is safe to move them. Yesenda, I fear William already suspects the truth, and it has been over a month since I had word from Brother Mateo."

"But how can I possibly do anything if I'm to wed? And who exactly has Ruadh promised me to?"

"Your brother intends to unite your clan to the Hendersons."

"Bram Henderson? He wants me to marry Bram? Absolutely not! I will not do it."

"Calm down. Bram is also reluctant to wed you. I believe he is smitten with Sorcha MacGregor, whom he kidnapped several weeks ago."

"He kidnapped Beiste MacGregor's sister?"

"Aye."

"What a fool! No man in their right mind would risk the ire of the Beast. Please Mother Abbess, I have not trained my whole life just to marry an idiot," Yesenda pleaded.

"If my sources are correct, I dinnae think you will have to marry anyone. Beiste MacGregor is none too happy, and I believe he and his war band are heading to Glencoe as we speak."

"Oh wonderful, so I am walking straight into a clan war thanks to bloody Ruadh!" Yesenda threw her hands up in the air and started pacing again. "Is it a sin to kill one's brother?"

"Lass! Would you sit down and stop pacing? You're making me dizzy."

"Sorry Mother Abbess. There is a lot to digest. I dinnae understand how you can think this helps the Order."

"The last missive Brother Mateo sent was from *Onich*."

"*Onich*? That is close to Henderson Keep."

"Aye, now do you ken why tis best you go."

"Oh... I see. But what of this blasted wedding? If I have to do all the betrothal things, how can I continue searching?"

"Have you learned nothing under my care?" The abbess raised her eyebrow and said, "Have I ever let you down?"

Yesenda cracked the first smile she had since she heard the dreadful news. The abbess was shrewd and meticulous in her planning. Finally, Yesenda relaxed. "No, you have never let me down, Mother Abbess."

"I have kenned you since you were a bairn. We have had many adventures together, so I ken you will escape the marriage. Trust me. All you need to do is smile prettily and pretend. Can you manage that?"

Yesenda sighed and said, "I suppose so."

"Good, because as much as it pains me to see you go, it is time for Miriam Ferguson to die and for Yesenda MacDonald to reclaim her rightful place in the world.

Henderson Keep - Two Weeks Later

YESENDA SAT IN THE Great Hall, having been formally welcomed by Laird Henderson and his family. The journey from the abbey to Henderson Keep went without incident, although her conversation with Ruadh was stilted. It had been fifteen years since she had seen her older brother and the playful young boy she remembered as a child had grown into a serious, contemplative man. He reminded her of her late father. Ruadh had a muscular physique and a commanding presence. He was the epitome of a leader. This was apparent, as every word he commanded was followed without question. She wondered about the weight of responsibilities thrust upon him at such an early age.

A part of her resentment faded as she tried to imagine being in his shoes. Ruadh would not have known how to handle a little sister. He had a clan to lead. It took the sting out of her feelings of abandonment. What she did not appreciate was how Ruadh treated her as if she was a fragile flower. He assumed she had been gently reared and could not ride a horse and he kept her protected within a circle of riders, which was stifling.

When their contingent arrived at Henderson Keep, it was with a lot of ceremony. Now she sat at the main table on the dais in the Great Hall.

Yesenda remained calm and continued to smile sweetly at all and sundry. She had to admit Bram Henderson had grown into a fine dashing braw highlander. He was a very handsome man with a commanding presence. But there was no spark between them. In fact, it was highly noticeable that Bram kept glaring at the beautiful young woman at the end of the table who was ignoring him in return. She sat beside one of her guardsmen. A man named Lachlan.

Yesenda sipped her drink to stifle her chuckle. It was just as the abbess said, Bram Henderson was besotted with his captive Sorcha MacGregor and from the chatter of servants the two were not behaving as a captor and captive should.

Yesenda decided she would do her part to move things along.

Yesenda asked, "Laird Henderson, what are you going to do about Sorcha? Surely you must release her to her family. I feel quite sorry for the lass."

Bram seemed stunned by her frank question. "That is between me and her brother."

"I doubt he will be very understanding. You have all but ruined the woman in the eyes of the church."

Bram flinched and frowned. "What do you mean?"

Yesenda casually sipped her wine and said, "Well, miss MacGregor has been here several weeks and when a woman is captured by a rival clan, it is common knowledge she may not return a maiden."

"Yesenda, dinnae speak of such things," Ruadh said with a warning tone.

"Oh, did I speak out of turn?" She feigned innocence.

"Tis all right. You were raised at the abbey and dinnae ken the way of things. Some matters are not openly discussed," Bram said.

"I apologize. I was just concerned about miss MacGregor's future chances of making a good marriage, now."

"Aye, I understand, but that is between me and Beiste MacGregor."

Yesenda changed tack. "Ruadh, why dinnae you marry miss MacGregor? She is quite bonnie, and I am sure you would make her a fine husband. Surely the MacGregor chieftain would not object. You ken each other, do you not?"

Ruadh half choked on his wine and started coughing at her suggestion.

Before he could respond, Bram pounded his fist on the table and said, "Sorcha is not marrying anyone! Her future is between me and her brother. Now if you will excuse me. Ruadh, I need a word."

Bram stood, waited for Ruadh to join him, then the men left, taking Lachlan with them.

Yesenda smirked into her wineglass.

When the men quit the hall Yesenda moved towards the woman she most wanted to speak to. She sat down beside Sorcha.

Sorcha was too stunned to speak. Yesenda had no such problem.

"I see the way he looks at you," Yesenda said.

"Who?" Sorcha asked.

"Bram."

"I dinnae ken what you mean."

"Do you not? Then mayhap you are the only one." Yesenda raised her eyebrow.

Sorcha blushed and said, "Bram is far too busy to bother with me."

"On the contrary. He looks at you with hunger. The type of expression I hope to garner from a man of my choosing someday."

"What do you mean? You have no choice, Yesenda. If you mean to cuckold Bram, you best think again!" Sorcha said vehemently.

Yesenda got the full measure of the woman. Sorcha was also desperately in love with Bram Henderson.

"As much as I respect Bram, I dinnae want to marry him and contrary to what most people think, including my brother, I have choices, Sorcha. We all do."

"Why are you telling me this?" Sorcha asked.

"I believe we can come to an arrangement."

"What sort of arrangement?"

"Mayhap you could take my place?"

"I think everyone would notice the difference," Sorcha scoffed.

"You are his lover, are you not?" Yesenda asked forthrightly.

"No, I ama captive held here against my will."

"Are you a captive Sorcha? Look around. You are not treated like a prisoner, but part of the clan. If you played your cards better, you may secure your heart's desire."

After exchanging a few more words, Yesenda took her leave. She knew Bram was not going to marry her. All she had to do now was stay out of the way.

Yesenda was so focused on her machinations she failed to realize she herself had become the object of someone else's undivided attention.

IAIN HENDERSON STOOD by the fireplace, quietly contemplating Yesenda MacDonald. From the moment she entered the Keep he could not take his eyes off her. It was a troubling thought for she was to become Bram's wife. Still, Iain found her enthralling. The word *'destiny'* came to mind as if the fates had whispered it to him.

Iain thought she was perfection. Then he clenched his fists. *Damn him*, she was off limits. He needed to stop staring, yet he could not tear his eyes away.

Iain watched Yesenda make her way back to the other side of the dais. She sat beside his niece and nephews. His niece Mysie wiggled her eyebrows at Yesenda. Iain watched with rapt attention as Yesenda crossed her eyes and stuck her tongue out at Mysie. Mysie giggled and made a face, and this went back and forth between them.

Iain grinned at the exchange.

For the first time in a long time, a woman other than Liosa captured Iain's attention. But he shook his head. She was as good as married to Bram, and it was not right to lust after his cousin's betrothed. Still, Iain continued to sip his whiskey by the fire and study her. There was something mysterious, almost secretive about her, and damn if that did not pique his interest enough that he wanted to find out what it was.

Iain wondered what it would be like to be with a woman like Yesenda. Gently reared in an abbey. No doubt he would scare the life out of her because he was not a gentle man. He thought she was most likely fragile, and he would need to handle her with care. Iain sighed. Yesenda was not for him.

He thought about Bram, whom he loved like a brother and was loyal to a fault. When Bram vied for the lairdship, Iain backed him, wanting nothing for himself. He wanted nothing for himself, only what was best for his clan. But for the first time in his entire life, Iain was jealous of his cousin.

Chapter 5

The Road Home – *One Week Later*

The MacDonald contingent made their way home after the betrothal fell through. As they rode along the road, Yesenda could barely hide her elation. True to form, she had eluded the marriage to Bram by simply staying out of everyone's way. She was just grinning to herself when Ruadh interrupted her reverie as he brought his horse beside hers.

"Yesenda, I am truly sorry. I hope you are not upset that the betrothal did not go ahead."

"Tis all right, brother. It was plain to see that Bram and Sorcha were smitten with each other. I am happy it is a love match for both and will keep the peace between their clans."

"You are very gracious, sister."

They rode on in silence as Ruadh seemed to contemplate something. "After what happened with Bram, I think you should have some time to settle back into our clan before I arrange a suitable match."

"That is a wise plan. I want to become better acquainted with our clan again. Brother, would you allow me to be frank?"

"Of course, sister. Share what is on your mind."

"I've lived behind abbey walls most of my life. I would like to get some time to understand the world. To enter marriage so soon would be confining. I would like to enjoy a little freedom for a while."

Ruadh nodded in understanding. "It must have been difficult reconciling the two worlds. I see your point sister and I can grant you your wish. There is no pressure from me and mayhap I will allow you some freedom to even choose your own match should the time come."

"You would? Really?"

"Aye, there is no pressing reason for any hasty weddings or alliances. However, there will be some considerations."

"Like what?"

"You cannot marry a pompous ass English man."

Yesenda grinned. "I doubt that will ever happen."

"And you cannot marry a Norseman and have his family settle here."

"Why not?"

"Good grief, have you not seen what happened in Normandy? The French let them stay and then they were overrun."

Yesenda just laughed. "Anything else?"

"Make sure the man you marry can protect you, Yesenda. I ken you are gently reared and violence is a strange concept to you, but I assure you, in a skirmish, you need a powerful man by your side. I fear you would break apart, having never seen what men are capable of."

"Aye, brother. You are wise." She smirked and tried not to laugh out loud. It was ludicrous that all the men she encountered assumed she was fragile. Yesenda just shrugged and let it wash over her.

"May I travel a little, see a bit of our fair country and visit friends from time-to-time?"

"Of course, Yesenda, I dinnae expect you to be a prisoner. Take a guardsman with you at all times."

MacDonald Keep

YESENDA AWOKE TO THE sounds of shouting. "Not again," she groaned and tried to muffle the sound with her pillow. It was no use. Her chamber was on the same floor as Ruadh's and again he was arguing with their guest.

"I told you I want to go home!" a woman shouted.

"And I told you, I will not allow it!" Ruadh bellowed.

"You cannot keep me here against my will, Ruadh MacDonald."

"I can if it keeps you out of harm's way."

"You are infuriating. Go away then and leave me be."

"Dinnae tell me what to do. Damn you, I am laird of this clan, and you will cease ordering me about."

"I will cease ordering you about when you stop yelling at me!" she shouted.

Yesenda went to her door. She yanked it opened and just shook her head at the sight. If her nerves were not so frayed from the amount of noise in the Keep, she would find it humorous to see her big brawny brother getting a blistering earful from a woman half his size. But after being woken several times to the sound of arguing, she found nothing funny about it.

"Would you both stop bellowing? The entire Keep can hear you."

"Be quiet!" they both yelled.

"Ruadh, leave her be. She clearly does not want to talk to you. And you," — She pointed at the woman — "Your kin sent you here for safekeeping. My brother is keeping his word to your da. If you dinnae like it, take it up with your da instead."

Yesenda slammed the door and stormed back to her bed. She did not know what was going on between Ruadh and the Boyd lass. Since she had returned home, Yesenda had not had a single moment of peace with the two of them constantly bickering. The place truly was in complete disarray when she arrived. It had taken Yesenda several days to set things to right. She missed life at the abbey where it was quiet and orderly.

SEVERAL DAYS LATER, Ruadh asked Yesenda if he could have a private word with her. When she entered Ruadh's chambers, she was struck by how much he resembled their late father. Other clan members commented on the fact that she resembled their late mother. How fitting that their parents left their own likeness behind in terms of feature and temperament.

"Yesenda, I am thinking of marrying."

"Really? Who is the fortunate woman?"

"I have none just yet, but several clans have requested that I consider their daughters and I think tis time I took a wife."

There was silence between them then Yesenda asked, "And what about miss Boyd, who you've now placed in mother's solar?"

Ruadh glance up at her and said dismissively, "She will remain here under my protection."

"Even after you marry?"

"Aye, I dinnae mean to cast her out."

"I doubt your wife would welcome another woman using her solar."

"My wife will do as I say. If miss Boyd needs to remain here for her own protection, then no one will gainsay me."

"But who is miss Boyd to you, Ruadh?" Yesenda asked.

"Tis none of your concern."

"You have feelings for her. Just admit it."

"No, I do not. She is the most annoying person I've ever met."

Yesenda watched him scowl after delivering that line.

"Just make sure you dinnae ruin her if there's nothing serious between you," she said.

"It's not like that between us. And if it was, it would still be none of your concern. You've been cloistered in an abbey all these years. I doubt you understand the world. I just wanted to inform you of my intentions so you dinnae hear it from anyone else."

"Aye, thank you for letting me ken your intentions, Ruadh. While I am here, I would also like to request that I be allowed to travel further afield. I am happy to take escorts with me but tis unnecessary if you cannot spare any men."

"Where would you like to go?"

"I may need to go to Normandy."

"Normandy! In France?"

"Aye brother, I would like to visit some friends from the abbey and—"

"No."

"What do you mean, no? You did not let me finish."

"Tis too far and with the trouble you attract, I doubt you'd reach there in one piece."

"Is this about what happened yestereve?" she asked.

"Aye it is."

"Ruadh, twas nothing but some mercenaries causing trouble over a misunderstanding."

"Yesenda, they almost killed you. Had it not been for the stranger who saved your life and then disappeared, I'd be planning your funeral today. What did you say the hero's name was again?"

"He did not state his name. He was passing by and saw me defenseless against those frightful men." Yesenda did not let on that there was no stranger, and she had defended herself. Ruadh would not believe her.

"No, tis decided. If you want to travel, make it closer to home. Now that I think on it, my men and I will escort miss Boyd to her brother's wedding. While I am away, you should visit Henderson Keep for a while. Mayhap it will be good to be with women your own age."

This worked in Yesenda's favor, so she agreed she would visit the Hendersons for a spell.

Chapter 6

1048 - Henderson Land, Scotland

Ian Henderson had an epiphany. He lounged in his bed with Liosa draped across him, pouting and giving him death glares. Something had changed between them, and he wondered why he was still doing this.

Liosa had turned up on his doorstep with a come-hither look. Iain had let her in against his better judgement. She jumped him the moment she was inside and removed his plaid. But Iain stopped her going any further.

That was then and now he lay on the bed staring up at the rafters while she whined because he refused to couple with her.

"Iain, my love, my body has missed your touch. Why are we lying on your bed doing nothing?"

Iain asked, "Liosa, where have you been these past three months?"

"I told you, I was in *Onich* visiting my kin."

"I went to *Onich* several days ago. You hadn't been there for months, they said."

Liosa, who was caressing his bare chest, sat up. "Have you been following me, Iain?" She scowled.

"Do I need to?"

She changed strategy and pouted, "Come now Iain, why so many questions? Does it really matter? Is it not enough that I'm back and I want to spend every waking moment with you?"

He looked skeptical, then said, "Then let me wed you, Liosa. Let me make a home for you." He was studying her expression closely and caught a flash of irritation in her eyes.

She whined, "Why must we always talk of marriage and the future? I am not ready to have bairns or be a commoner in some backwater town. I lead a busy life."

"Where? You never seem to tell me anything anymore."

"Someday I will settle but for now I prefer to travel and see my kin. The Hendersons are not my clan."

Iain said, "Then, if it means so much to you, I will join you."

She paused, then replied, "I am not ready, Iain. I thought I made it clear. We want different things."

"The man who gives you these fine garments is he the one you want to marry?" Iain bunched up her chemise, which was made of fine silk.

"Dinnae be daft! There is no man. Has it ever occurred to you I can make money for myself? You are quite feudal in your thinking, and that is a constant issue between us."

"Why is that an issue?" Iain frowned.

"Because you're so simple. You're wasting your life in this stupid glen, not even trying to reach for something more than this stupid place." Her hand waved about the cottage.

"You think me living in my home, on my land, making an honest living protecting my clan is... stupid?"

Liosa was off the bed and pacing in her see through chemise.

"Aye, Iain! It is stupid. You can at least aspire to become a nobleman or work for a king. You can be anything you want to be. Yet you choose this... life." She spat out the words as if his life were meaningless.

And there lay the problem. Iain realized no matter what he did, he would never be good enough for Liosa.

"Then if you dinnae want to marry me or have this life, why do you fall upon my shaft half-starved every time you see me? You need to be careful, Liosa, you could end up with child."

"Wheesht tis not possible, I ensure I take a herb to prevent it. No other man makes me feel as good as you do."

"There are others?" Iain said.

Liosa stilled and her eyes widened at her slip up. It was enough to confirm to Iain that he was a damned fool.

Iain leaped out of the bed. He fastened his plaid and threw his leine back on. He needed air, and he needed away from the woman who had played his heart strings his entire adult life.

"Iain, what are you doing? Where are you going?"

"Elsewhere. I have much to do."

"But you haven't even made love to me yet!"

"I've changed my mind, Liosa. I think you need to seek satisfaction from one of the *others*!"

"Iain dinnae be ridiculous. You are jumping to conclusions. Come to bed and stop fighting."

"Sorry, Liosa, but I dinnae think I can stomach bedding you, now or ever."

"What? You've never turned me down before!" she shrieked.

"There is a first time for everything. I have duties to see to." He buckled the last rung of his belt and reached for his scabbard, then walked towards the door.

She snorted, "Aye, go follow your cousin Bram around like a puppy dog. Honestly, you're as daft as your stupid cousins!"

Iain froze. In a voice laced with steel, he said, "Dinnae ever speak about Bram that way. He is my kin. He protected me after Cruim near beat me to death for challenging him for the lairdship."

"You should have beat that fat turd, instead you lost because you're useless!" she shouted.

"And where were you when I lost? Where were you when my broken body was bedridden, Liosa? You disappeared. Twas my family and this wee backwater clan who stood by me in my darkest days. But *my* woman, whom I loved, abandoned me!" he yelled.

Iain paused as if saying these things out loud gave him clarity for the first time.

"This is not my clan. I told you I have things to do which dinnae involve you," Liosa snapped.

"Why are you back, Liosa? Is it so you can ride my cock and seek your pleasure, then leave again?"

"Dinnae be so vulgar, Iain. You're daft."

"Then what? You never want to spend time with me outside of bed and half the time you're complaining about something I've done, then you're gone again. So why now? Why are you back here?"

"I told you. I still love you Iain and in time I will settle, just not now."

"You talk of love, Liosa, but you dinnae ken what it is."

"Oh, this again. Please enlighten me, Iain."

"My cousin Willa, my sister Tyra, my aunt Fia stayed up with me tending to my injuries the night Cruim nearly killed me. Bram and Niall took on my responsibilities at the Keep. The clan made sure I had food in my belly and enough firewood for the winter, because I was too weak to hunt or wield an axe. Why? Because that's what kin do when they love you. My life may be stupid to you, Liosa, but it means the world to me, and I'll not have you disparage it."

"My goodness, you talk about your family as if they're bloody saints, for crying out loud. I am sick of you talking about your wretched clan."

"I feel sorry for you, Liosa."

"Why?"

"Because you've spent your whole life chasing things that hold no real value. Keep your fine garments and pursue your wealthy kings. I hope they make you happy."

There was silence between them, then Liosa moved towards him. Her voice softened. She wrapped her arms around his waist, then she moved her hand lower and began stroking him beneath his plaid. Her voice was husky and soft, almost demure. "Please dinnae let's fight. You ken how much I need you, Iain. I love you truly, I do, but I need time. Come back to bed, and we can do something more agreeable?"

Usually, Iain would jump at the chance to bed her, but this time, he grabbed her wrist and pushed it away.

"No, Liosa. I think tis time you returned to wherever it is you go. When I come back, I want you gone."

"But I need to stay in *Glencoe* longer. I have nowhere else to go."

"Then do what you must. But you'll not stay in my cottage. Willa's is empty. You can stay there."

He opened the door and turned his head when she called out.

"Iain? Are you really refusing to couple with me?" She had an incredulous look on her face.

"Aye, believe it."

"But it has been months!" she shouted.

He just shrugged.

Then the air in the cottage changed, and Liosa grabbed his arm to turn him to face her. This time, her eyes were squinty. "Who is she, Iain? Are you swiving someone else? Is that why you dinnae want me anymore? I swear Iain when I find out who it is—"

"There is no one, Liosa. Unlike you, I dinnae work that way."

So you really dinnae want me, and you're kicking me out of your cottage?"

"Aye. I dinnae think we should keep coupling if there is no serious intention beyond it. I've asked you to marry me three times and you refuse, so I dinnae think there's anything more to it."

"And that's it? You're breaking off our courtship?"

"What courtship, Liosa? You will not even acknowledge a relationship, which is why we keep sneaking about!" he yelled.

"I honestly dinnae ken what has gotten into you, Iain. You have been nothing but grumpy since I arrived. I thought a good swiving would improve your mood but clearly not."

Iain just shook his head. "Move into Willa's cottage. And steer clear of the Henderson women. They dinnae like you." With those parting words, Iain left his cottage and slammed the door behind him.

As he walked past the window, Liosa yelled out, "Wait, Iain! I wanted to ask you something."

"What?" he growled.

"Do you ken a lass by the name of Ferguson?"

"No. Why?"

"Oh, tis just a dear old friend I would like to reconnect with."

Iain just shook his head and kept walking. Trust Liosa to change subjects when it suited her.

Iain went to the river, stripped off, and plunged into the freezing cold. He needed to purge himself of the unpleasant morning. As he scrubbed himself clean, he had to admit the pleasures Liosa offered him no longer satisfied. It only caused him more frustration and regret. At least this time, he did not have to beat himself up for sleeping with her. That was a first, considering he had never abstained from finding pleasure with Liosa.

As Iain got out of the water and dried himself, he realized he was indeed changing. He wanted something more than empty promises and heartache.

WHEN IAIN ARRIVED AT the Keep the place was in a frenzy. "What is going on?" he asked a serving woman as she flew past him.

"The MacDonald lass is coming to stay."

"When?"

"Today."

Iain frowned. Wondering where she was going to sleep, seeing as Sorcha's entire family was also visiting. Sorcha's sister-in-law Amelia MacGregor was a gifted healer, and she was insistent that she help with the delivery of Sorcha's babe. Sorcha's other sisters-in-law, Zala Fletcher and Clarissa Robertson wanted to be there as well. Their husbands, Beiste MacGregor, Brodie Fletcher and Dalziel Robertson refused to allow the women to travel alone, so they came with their bairns in tow. Henderson Keep was currently overrun with boisterous MacGregors.

It was the first Iain heard about Yesenda joining them as well. For some inextricable reason, his heart started pounding in excitement. He hastened his steps, making his way to the main hall where he knew his laird and cousins would be.

He entered and took a seat beside his cousin Niall.

"What's this I hear about the MacDonalds joining us as well?"

"They're arriving today. Yesenda will remain with us until Ruadh, and his men return from escorting some lass to *Ayrshire*. I swear, cousin, this place is being overrun by loud, bossy women. I dinnae ken how Bram puts up with it," Niall grumbled.

Iain chuckled and said, "I'm sure when you find a bonnie lass to marry, you'll put up with her family as well."

"No, I will not. I will never marry. Not if this is what I have to look forward to. I'd rather run naked through a meadow with *urisks* and howl at the moon like old Duff Henderson."

Iain just grinned and shook his head.

AS PROMISED, RUADH and his men escorted Yesenda to Henderson Keep before continuing on with their journey. But before he took his leave, Ruadh cautioned Bram. They were in Bram's meeting room when he broached the subject.

"Thank you for agreeing to host my sister for a short time. I feel better that she will have good female company."

"Tis our pleasure. Yesenda gets on well with my wife, Sorcha, and my family. It will be a welcome addition. How has she adjusted to life outside the abbey?" Bram asked.

"She is adjusting slowly. I would feel better if she were married to a man who could protect her. I am a little regretful you did not wed her. Although I can see you are thrilled with your bride."

"I regret what happened, but I would not give up Sorcha for the world. But why does Yesenda need protection?"

"Since she returned from the abbey there have been several strange mishaps and tis only by the grace of God has my sister survived them."

"What mishaps?"

"Well, she was on her way to the priory last sennight to deliver alms for the poor. But on the way, she was thrown from her horse and almost crushed by a moving cart."

"That is dire indeed."

"When my men came to her rescue there was a dead man on the roadside. Yesenda said the man was trying to help her when he was trampled to death."

"Who was the man?" Bram asked.

"That's the thing. I'd never seen him before. He was no farmer from our region, or a tinker of some sort, and his cart held no goods for barter."

Bram furrowed his brow, thinking it was strange indeed. "And what else?"

"Then last month, she asked to go to a festival nearby. Of course, I let her go. I sent guardsmen with her and apparently something happened in the village that night."

"What?"

"Yesenda was at an inn. She wanted fresh water and did not want to wake the innkeeper. So, she went to the well to fetch the water and almost fell in. A man tried to rescue her, but he got caught up in the rope and drowned," Ruadh said.

"That is strange indeed."

"Again no one could confirm the identity of the man because he was not from the village."

"Mayhap your sister is very clumsy or just attracts trouble."

"Aye, I cannot help but think that she is a walking disaster. I worry because she is innocent being sheltered at the abbey that if she's not careful, someone could really harm her."

"Dinnae worry, Ruadh, we will keep an eye on her, seeing as she is most likely completely helpless in the ways of the world. I'll ensure she remains guarded."

"Thank you. I will fetch her when I return."

"And what of marriage? Have you lined someone up for her?" Bram asked.

Ruadh shook his head. "I see no need to rush things."

"Aye, she is still young."

"And how fares Iain and your brother, Niall?" Ruadh asked.

"Both are still unmarried. Niall is currently sowing his wild oats across *Alba*, I assume, and Iain, well he is still very stubborn and set in his ways."

"What of that god awful woman, Liosa?"

Bram sighed. "She is still around. She comes and goes. Wreaks havoc with his life, then leaves again."

"I dinnae ken why they dinnae just marry. They have been dancing around each other for years."

"Well, tis not for want of Iain asking. He has offered for her hand several times, but she is opposed to the union."

"What do you think of her, Bram?"

I dinnae like her because I dinnae like the person Iain becomes when she is around. She leads him on a merry dance with no proper concern for his feelings. He deserves better. He is a good man."

Then Bram asked Ruadh, "What of you? Do you have plans to marry?"

"Aye, I have been thinking about it of late."

"When the time is right, you will find the woman of your dreams just like I did... and kidnap her."

Ruadh paused, then chuckled while Bram grinned at him.

"I'll be sure the woman I fall for has no brothers who want to beat me to death."

Bram shrugged. "I'm just saying it worked for me. I have a beauty in my bed with a bairn on the way. And god's teeth, I love her. Twas the best decision I ever made."

"I am happy for you, Bram. But a part of me still wishes you married Yesenda and took her mishaps off my hands."

"Och, come on now. How much trouble can your little sister be?"

Chapter 7

Henderson Keep

When the MacDonalds arrived, there was an air of excitement, especially as the three clans would all be together. They gathered everyone in the hall, as there was a special feast prepared for the new arrivals.

Iain sat at a trestle table along the side of the hall. He felt a nervous energy flow through him as he waited for their arrival.

Ruadh MacDonald approached the dais first, and a young woman accompanied him. She appeared reluctant to sit at the main table and moved to sit at a trestle table below. But in front of everyone, Ruadh grabbed her hand and pulled her to sit beside him. She flashed an annoyed glare, then shuffled down the bench away from him. Ruadh reached out, placed his arm around the woman's waist, and dragged her back until she was plastered to his side. Then Ruadh completely ignored her.

Iain wondered what was happening between them when he felt the air in the room shift. He knew, deep down inside without seeing her, he *felt* the moment Yesenda entered the hall.

Iain slowly turned his head and there she was, walking down the center of the hall in a long purple kirtle with a surcoat. The outfit clung to her lithe figure. Her sandy blonde locks hung loose down her back. To Iain she walked like an ethereal creature as she moved with grace. He had to take a moment to catch his breath. He felt like someone had punched him in the gut, such was the impact of her mere presence.

It was the same feeling he felt months ago, except back then Yesenda was off limits. She was betrothed to Bram, but this time, she belonged to no man. He held his gaze steady upon her and nothing else mattered in that moment. Yesenda had him enthralled.

Mine! said that voice in his head.

Iain willed Yesenda to look at him as if his very life depended on it. Then it happened. Yesenda walked past and slowly turned her head and stared directly at Iain. She blinked languidly, and her face filled with warmth as her lips curved upwards. Yesenda gave him a brief nod, then she winked at him before looking ahead and stepping up onto the dais.

Iain's face split into a wide grin. He wanted to roar and beat his chest.

"Iain? Have you heard anything I've said?" He heard someone speak beside him and his entire mood shattered. It surprised him to see Liosa moving to his side. *She never came to clan gatherings.*

"Iain, my love? What are you grinning about?"

Iain's face shuttered, and his smile turned into a frown. "Liosa? What are you doing here?"

"I thought about what you said. And you're right. I need to make more effort with your family. If that's what it will take to prove my love, then I will do it."

"Liosa, I dinnae need you to prove anything—"

"Iain, please. Things are not well for me right now and I dinnae want us to fight." She wove her arm through his and sat closer to him. "Let's just share a peaceful meal together, please?"

"Aye," he said. Although he pulled his arm out of hers and served separate trenchers for them. He was hit by another first. Iain wished Liosa would leave him alone.

YESENDA SAT ON THE main table on the dais, maintain a nonchalant expression. She quietly listened to the conversation around her and smiled, but rarely joined in. Yesenda learned that one could glean far more information by being a ready listener as opposed to a talker. Yesenda found the Henderson and MacGregor women rather amusing. There was a friendly rapport between them with no pretense, and she enjoyed their lively company. Sorcha's sisters-in-law, Amelia, Zala and Clarissa were hilarious when they were together because they kept plotting and scheming.

Yesenda sipped her wine whilst her eyes scanned the hall for any signs of danger. It was a safety measure she developed over the years. But repeatedly, her eyes would settle back on Iain Henderson. She had to admit he truly was a handsome man. There was a rugged masculinity to Iain that she liked. But it was his eyes that enchanted. They were dark and intense, but there was a kindness in them. He had faint laugh lines around the sides, and she longed to hear him laugh. She snuck surreptitious glances his way several times during the meal and she wondered who the woman was beside him. There was an intimacy between them, and logic dictated that she must be Iain's lover.

Yesenda sighed at the realization because an unwelcome feeling stole over her. It was *envy*. She wondered what type of lover Iain would make, then blushed at her errant thought. She had no business lusting after a man she could not have. Her path was chosen long ago. The work Yesenda carried out for the *Order* was dangerous, and she could not afford emotions to detract from her mission. Yesenda tried to find something else to focus on. That's when she saw him.

It was a quick glance, but she knew who it was. A lean built lad wearing a hooded garment sat among the keep staff. Yesenda glared at him when their eyes met, and she saw the shock register on his face at being caught. She knew he was going to run, so she politely excused herself from the present company, feigning a need for fresh air. Yesenda moved down the side of the dais. She smiled sweetly at passers-by, then quickened her pace. As soon as she hit the dimly lit passageway, she bolted past the guards and straight out into the night. Her plan was to cut off his escape route.

Yesenda had read his movements correctly and spotted the hooded figure running across the bailey. She took off after him. Climbing up the turret, she timed the moment and jumped down, landing in front of him.

She pulled off his hood and scolded him. "Edmund! Do you ken how dangerous it is to be here?"

"Aww, but I just wanted to join the festivities," he whined.

She grabbed his arm and dragged him around the corner near the shrubbery.

"What have I told you about staying away from large gatherings?"

"But I'm never allowed to go anywhere."

"I've told you before, there's a reason. Tis only temporary, you must remain out of sight until an escort arrives from Brother Mateo. You ken there are men who wish you dead, Edmund?"

"But I have done nothing wrong."

"Where are your foster parents?"

"Tis just me. I snuck out when they went to market."

"Are you daft?" Yesenda took deep breaths to calm herself. She needed to remember he was just a curious young lad who did not know the threat he posed to the Duke of Normandy.

"Where is your guard, then? I want to have a stern word with him."

Edmund said, "I... I could not find him to ask."

"Well, I am going to see you home and make sure you remain there."

"Aw, can't I just stay for a little while?"

"I am sorry, Edmund, but you cannot. I promise in the future you will have far more freedom, but I need you to be patient and trust me, please."

He sighed heavily as one who carried the weight of the world on his shoulders. "All right."

Ballachullish Township

IT HAD TAKEN YESENDA some maneuvering to get away from Henderson Keep unnoticed. But she managed it. She had also changed into trews and her cloak, which had several weapons hiding within the seams.

By the time Yesenda and Edmund reached the top of the road leading to the cottage where Edmund and his foster parents lived, it was close to midnight. She surveyed the cottage. There was light shining inside and smoke coming from the chimney. A guard sat outside in a chair. Everything looked as it should except her instincts told her all was not normal.

She quickly grabbed the reins of Edmund's mount, stopping its progress.

Yesenda whispered, "Edmund, dismount now and move your horse to the trees. Do it quickly."

Sensing the tension, Edmund did as she asked.

She followed suit and moved her horses into a copse of trees.

"Take this." She handed him a knife. "Do you ken how to use it?"

"Aye," he said. "Brother Mateo taught me."

"Good, then keep it close and remain hidden and wait for me."

"Has something happened to my parents?" Edmund asked with a worried expression.

"I dinnae ken, but I will find out."

"Then I will come and help you—"

"No, you will stay put. No matter what happens or whatever you hear, you remain hidden. Do you hear me?"

He sighed and nodded, then moved to crouch behind the shrubbery.

"Should anything happen to me, you ken where to go?"

Edmund nodded.

"Good." Her expression softened when she squeezed his arm and said, "Stay safe, Edmund."

"You too, Yesenda."

Yesenda lifted the hood of her black cloak over her head and then sprinted along the tree line the remaining one hundred yards under the cover of darkness. She continued to scan her surroundings, not wanting to walk into an ambush. As she approached the cottage, she was grateful she listened to her instincts because the guard was not asleep. He was dead and propped up against the chair. His head caved in. She moved towards the window and peered inside. Edmunds foster parents were tied up with gags over their mouths. They looked beaten and bruised.

Beside the door stood a man wielding a war club. No doubt lying in wait for Edmund to come home. She peered at his garment and noted the cut and hue.

Yesenda crouched back down with her back against the cottage. She recognized the garment. They were usually worn by monks belonging to the French *Order of Tiron*. They were *Grey Monks*. But she was confused because they were a peaceful order. They would never kill or wield war clubs against a young lad.

She heard the rustling of leaves as she tried to figure out what to do next. Yesenda whipped her head to the side and saw Edmund creeping his way towards the cottage. She glared at him and gestured using hand signals, demanding he go back and hide. But the stubborn lad ignored her.

Edmund was making too much noise, and it was only a matter of time before the monk caught sight of him.

Sure enough, she heard the front door open and footsteps running toward Edmund. The lad froze as the looming figure of the monk stood before him. Edmund raised his knife, but it would be no match for a war club. Just as the monk brought the club crashing down, Yesenda yanked Edmund out of the way, narrowly missing getting hit.

"Go inside and help your parents, now!" she demanded in a voice that brooked no opposition. Edmund headed for the front door.

The monk appeared startled by Yesenda's appearance. He said, "You must be Miriam Ferguson. We have been searching for you."

She still did not know who he was, but she would fight first and ask questions later.

The monk spun the club around and aimed it at her with all his might. Yesenda reached behind her and pulled out her mace. The weapons clashed, making a loud thudding sound. She stepped back and pivoted as he advanced with a fast succession of hits. He was on the attack and Yesenda maintained her defensive moves, weaving and dodging, blocking, and parrying each blow. She shifted quickly from side to side.

The monk was adept at his weapon, but she had taken his measure. He was not as fit as he thought he was, and the slight labored panting gave him away. She knew in time he would tire. War clubs were heavy and his was wrought with iron.

They circled one another.

The monk tried to provoke her.

"You are beautiful *mademoiselle*. I will enjoy rutting inside you until you bleed. You will beg for death," he said.

"Is that the only way you can get a woman? By maiming her. Mayhap tis because you have a small cock?"

A flash of anger marred his features, and he upped his hits. They were becoming uncoordinated.

"Oh, I appear to have touched a nerve. Tis true then? Your penis is small, *no?*"

He roared and moved in again with a rapid succession of hits. Each one she blocked or dodged.

"I will make sure I keep you alive long enough for all my brothers to enjoy you, too. We will rip you in half with our large phalluses."

Yesenda chuckled. "That is something a man with a tiny-wee cock would say."

"You, bitch!" he snarled and went on the attack again.

Yesenda secretly smiled. He was tiring much faster. Anger truly was the enemy of reason.

She took a step back and made a slight misstep, stumbling backward. The monk aimed to take advantage. He swung high. Yesenda managed to roll out of the way. The sharp end of the club sliced her arm, but it was not deep.

Yesenda rolled into a crouch position, then she ran at him. He was not expecting the move, and he tried to run backwards but tripped on his own robe and lost his balance. It was the advantage she needed. When he went down, he dropped the club. Yesenda picked it up. She now held a weapon in each hand.

The monk was back on his feet, and he roared in anger and rushed at her.

Yesenda spun both weapons and brought them both crashing down across his middle. He screamed in pain and hit the ground, writhing in agony. She placed a foot on his neck and asked, "Who sent you? Where are your brothers?"

His eyes rolled to the back of his head, and he passed out from the pain. Yesenda shook her head and removed her foot.

Edmund's foster parents, Sienna and Gideon, came running outside. They told Yesenda that the monk said there were others already in the village.

"Then you need to leave tonight and move to the next haven we discussed."

"Aye," Gideon nodded.

"Will you come with us?" Sienna asked.

"Not yet. I will remain to flush out the others, buy you some time, then I will join you. Pack everything and I'll burn the cottage to the ground. I'll tie up the monk—"

Before Yesenda could finish her sentence, Gideon pulled out a dagger and sliced the monk's throat.

Yesenda was about to protest when Gideon said, "He kens too much, he beat a lot of information out of us, and he has seen *all* our faces. Even yours. We cannot let him live."

Yesenda nodded and made the sign of the cross.

Then they set about putting their plan into place.

The next morning Edmund and his parents were gone, and news spread of a burnt-out cottage with the remains of the unfortunate owner amidst the carnage.

Yesenda returned to the Keep at pre-dawn. She changed back into a dress in the stables, being sure to stuff everything into a knapsack. By the time she re-entered the Keep, she was so exhausted she crept into the first empty bed chamber she could find and then slept like the dead.

THAT NIGHT IAIN LAY awake in his cottage by the glen, alone and staring at the rafters. He wondered what happened to Yesenda after the meal in the hall. He tried to find her, but Liosa would not leave his side. Seeing as the Henderson women really did not like Liosa, he spent the entire night running interference before his sister Tyra and cousin Willa scratched Liosa's eyes out. All he thought about was Yesenda, her warm smile, and a wink. He wondered how he could get close to her. Iain's thoughts were interrupted by a knock at the door.

"Iain? My love? Are you still awake? I cannot sleep."

He ignored Liosa. She banged louder.

"Go away, Liosa. Nothing has changed. Tis best we keep our distance."

"Please, Iain, I just dinnae want to sleep alone. Tis cold."

"Then light a damned fire."

"I dinnae ken how to," she whined.

"Bloody hell!" he grumbled. Iain threw open the door and stormed past her to Willa's old cottage. Once inside, he went about lighting a fire in the hearth. Iain sensed Liosa hovering behind him, but did not look until the fire was burning. He added an extra log, then stood and made for the door.

"Iain. Please sleep with me tonight. I need to feel you inside me."

When he turned Liosa was fully naked with a sultry look on her face.

Iain clenched his jaw, feeling torn. He had abstained from sexual relations for a long time. He would be lying if he said he felt nothing physically. But he was not eager as he had been in the past. He clenched his fists as he felt Liosa's soft hands caress his bare chest. This is how she worked her way back into his life.

Iain took a deep breath and closed his eyes. Then the strangest thing happened. The images in his head were not of a naked Liosa, but Yesenda winking at him. He opened his eyes immediately, and he stepped away from Liosa.

Iain just shook his head and said, "You need to learn to sleep alone, Liosa."

Iain walked out of the cottage and shut the door behind him. Leaving a shocked Liosa behind.

When he was back in his cottage staring at the rafters again, he thought about how Liosa still could not light her own fire, or even make breakfast or cook or clean, or do anything that required work or effort. He wondered why she had never learned. *How did the woman survive?* For as long as he could remember in their relationship, he did everything. He chopped wood, hunted for game, and cooked their meals. He even baked fresh bread for her when she had a craving. Liosa never shared any of the chores. *How did he not notice that before?*

It seemed as if he was having a book of revelations season. When Iain finally fell asleep, images of sandy blonde locks and a mischievous wink replaced all his worries.

Chapter 8

The following morning, Yesenda went to the river to bathe and wash her garments. The smell of fire and ash clung heavily to them. Yesenda picked a secluded spot and spent ample time scrubbing herself clean. She used a scented soap made with flower petals and rinsed out her hair. Little did she know while she was frolicking in the water, back at the Keep, she was the focus of several conversations.

"Has anyone seen Yesenda this morn?" Niall asked when he entered the hall. Iain and the MacGregor men sat together while the MacGregor women and children were spending time with Sorcha in her solar.

The men all shook their heads.

"Why are you looking for her?" Iain asked.

"I've come by some concerning news. I'll wait until Bram gets here to discuss it with you all."

Iain grew tense and impatient, waiting for Bram to arrive.

It was not long before Bram appeared with Lachlan, one of the MacGregor retainers.

"What is the matter?" Bram asked.

"Have either of you seen Yesenda this morn?" Niall asked.

"Why?" Bram asked.

"There is talk of a stranger. He has been asking about a lass from the abbey. He did not mention Yesenda's name but described her likeness."

Bram furrowed his brow. "We must be cautious. Ruadh asked me to keep an eye on her while she was here."

"Is she in danger?" Iain asked with concern.

63

"Ruadh mentioned that wherever his sister is, she attracts trouble."

"What kind of trouble?" Beiste MacGregor asked.

Bram disclosed what Ruadh said about Yesenda's mishaps. "I think someone needs to keep watch over the stranger and Yesenda needs to be guarded every time she leaves the Keep," Bram said.

"I'll do it," Iain said.

"Are you sure? You dinnae have to if you're busy—"

"I said, I'll do it."

"I'll ensure my guards are on alert when they watch over our women and bairns," Beiste MacGregor said.

"Does anyone ken where Yesenda is right now?" Niall asked.

Lachlan said, "Aye, I saw her outside my chamber this morn."

Iain frowned. "Why was she close to your chamber? There's no reason for her to be there."

Lachlan shrugged his shoulders. "All I ken is she was there this morn, then she was not there."

"Has anyone seen her since?"

They all shook their heads.

"I'll go find her," Iain said. He was rising from his seat when the woman in question breezed in, seemingly without a care in the world. Iain had to admit, she looked lovely.

"Yesenda," Bram said. "May we have a word with you?"

As she walked over to the men, she said, "Of course, laird."

Yesenda stood beside Iain, and he inhaled deeply, drinking in not just the sight of her, but also the scent of her skin. *She smells like fresh flowers.* Iain momentarily closed his eyes and savored the scent. It caused a heady sensation. When he opened his eyes, Bram was staring at him with a raised eyebrow.

"Is anything the matter?" Yesenda asked.

"Aye, there was a stranger asking about you in the village. Do you ken anyone from the village?"

"No, what does he look like?"

Niall said, "Male, medium height with fair hair, blue eyes and he dressed like a pilgrim. He had markings on his forearm.

"What kind?" she asked.

"Twas a spiked war club."

Yesenda frowned, then schooled her features. "I am at a loss. I ken nothing."

Bram said, "I will make more inquiries. In the meantime, you are to remain close to the Keep. Iain will accompany you if you need to go beyond the gates."

Yesenda protested, "Laird, tis unnecessary really. I am certain Iain has far more pressing concerns to—"

"You'll not leave this Keep without me, and that's final," Iain commanded.

Yesenda glanced at the men and could see none would relent, so she took the path of least resistance and agreed. "Of course, I thank ye, Laird, and Iain; I will notify you if I leave the Keep."

Iain nodded and continued to gaze at her with those dark, intense eyes.

Yesenda felt slightly disconcerted. She needed to set some distance between them. "If that is all, might I eat now?"

"Of course, thank you, Yesenda." Bram said.

She turned to walk away when Iain said, "Wait, I have not eaten yet, either. I will join you." It was a statement and not as a request. Iain then moved to her side and lightly placed his hand on her back, ushering her to a separate table.

"Ah... all right then." Yesenda felt like a wooden statue, slightly nervous about being in Iain's presence. She felt goose bumps on her skin.

Iain nodded and gestured for her to take a seat beside him for the meal. Yesenda complied.

When the food was served, she closed her eyes and quietly murmured something before she ate. When she opened her eyes, she felt Iain's gaze upon her again. She paused, as there was something indecipherable in his expression. It was warmth and softness directed at her.

"What were you doing?" Iain asked.

"Giving thanks," she replied.

"For your food?"

She blushed. "Aye. Sometimes in the abbey, food was scarce. I've learned to give thanks when I have it." She took a massive bite of the pie. "Oh my, this is the best pie I have ever tasted," she groaned as she chewed, utterly oblivious to the effect her words had on the listener.

Iain observed the way she savored the pie, then for the first time in a long time, he smiled, and this time, it reached his eyes.

He said a quick grace over his trencher, smiled and dug into his meal.

And it was over a simple meal of meat pie and cider that a friendship formed between them.

Iain realized Yesenda was a very interesting woman to talk to. Her perception of the world was refreshing, and he smiled a lot. He even burst out laughing at one of her stories from the abbey. She did not realize it, but Iain thought she was a natural storyteller. She would mimic voices and make facial expressions of subjects she was talking about, like a bard.

It was no surprise that soon his niece Mysie and nephews Michael and Domhnall joined them, including some of the MacGregor children. Iain watched Yesenda effortlessly include them all as she became even more animated with her storytelling. She had their rapt attention.

"And then what happened?" Mysie asked with her eyes wide open.

Yesenda replied, "Well, she lulled the *Each-Uisge* to sleep by running her fingers through his water weeds and muddy hair. She sat by the loch watching the fire burning and she kept her nerve. She did not want to get carried away into the deep waters and have her flesh torn from her bones."

Mysie gasped and shook her head. "Aye, that would not be very nice."

Yesenda continued as the children quietened down. "Finally, when the creature fell asleep, he revealed his true form. He was not a handsome braw man at all but the deadly water horse. She quietly inched her body away from the fire and the loch and ran for her life!"

"She was wise and very clever," Izara Fletcher said in awe. Izara was Brodie Fletcher's daughter, and the story enthralled her.

"And what do you think the lesson of the story is?" Yesenda asked.

"Never trust a braw man, especially if he tries to tear the flesh off your bones," Iona MacGregor said. The other children chuckled.

Iain glanced at Yesenda and grinned.

"I ken what the lesson is," Mysie said.

"Go on, tell us," Yesenda encouraged her.

"A lass should only court an ugly man with short hair and small teeth."

They all burst out laughing at her comment.

"What is the moral of the story, Yesenda?" Iain asked when they had all quietened down.

"You can never tell what a person's true nature is just by looking at them and when you face danger, you must remain calm and not let fear control you." Yesenda smiled as the children started nodding their heads.

At that moment, Iain felt his heart fill with so much warmth he thought it might explode with the depth of feeling he was experiencing. He just continued to gaze at Yesenda.

Yesenda could not remember the last time she shared such an enjoyable meal in such good company. It was one of the most pleasurable experiences of her life.

Iain was an easy conversationalist and had so much knowledge about the area and the clans. But it was the way he spoke of his kin with such love and loyalty, that won her over and the way he did not balk when Mysie jumped up on his lap and ate some of his pie. But what she enjoyed the most was seeing him laugh and his eyes fill with warmth. It was a beautiful thing to behold. It was in those moments Yesenda forgot about the burdens that came with being a keeper of secrets.

These Ordinary Moments

THE FOLLOWING AFTERNOON, Yesenda walked within the grounds of the Keep. She found it too noisy to sleep, given creaky floorboards and adjusting to new surrounds.

It was while she was in the courtyard that she felt a familiar presence.

"Yesenda?"

"Hello, Iain."

"I thought it was you. Where are you headed?"

"I was hoping to get some fresh air and familiarize myself with the area."

"Do you mind if I join you?" Iain asked.

"Not at all."

As they continued their walk, she asked, "How was your day, Iain?"

"It was good, thank you."

As Iain thought more about it, he realized that Liosa never asked him about his day. They were frolicking in bed or engaged in a row outside of it. There was no in-between.

"Did you do anything out of the ordinary or find something enjoyable?" Yesenda asked.

He paused and wondered that no one had asked him that before.

"Aye, I trained some of the new lads who foster with us for the summer," he replied.

"Do you enjoy training the young ones?"

"I do. There is something satisfying about being able to nurture and build on their natural talent. When you see them struggle to master something, then one day it all makes sense. Tis a great feeling of achievement."

Yesenda smiled at him as if she understood exactly what he meant. "That is a very meaningful thing indeed, Iain. To pass on your skills and wisdom to the next lot of warriors. It is as if you are preparing them for a time when you are not there."

"Aye, tis exactly as you say. They must learn to survive without us and that is why I am hard on them, because someday it could save their life."

"Tis a blessing, Iain, when you can prepare young ones for the future, even if you may not be around to see it. Tis a powerful legacy to leave behind," Yesenda said.

Iain felt a deep connection to her words and, not for the first time, it had him thinking about the legacy he would like to leave behind. Suddenly, he had visions of Yesenda ripe with his child in her belly and a home filled with love and stories by the fireplace. Another epiphany hit him.

"Good lord!" he said out loud.

"What is it?" Yesenda asked.

"Tis you, just you and... *this*. These ordinary moments made perfect because I get to share them with you," Iain whispered.

Yesenda blushed. "Iain, are you a bard perchance, because I think you just scribed the beginnings of a song?"

Iain paused for a moment, then threw his head back and burst out laughing. Yesenda took a sharp breath at the sheer beauty of it.

When Iain finally stopped laughing, his expression became wistful, and he said, "I've never met anyone like you, lass."

"Nor I you, Iain."

"Then we make a fine pair indeed." His heated gaze settled on her lips.

They both just stared at one another and did not move or speak. It felt almost intimate.

"Yesenda, is there a man in your life?" Iain needed to know.

"How do you mean?"

"Are you betrothed or courting anyone?"

"No, I am not. Why?"

"I just wanted to make sure. I'm sorry but I have to go. There is something important I need to see to."

"All right."

The next minute Iain was gone, and it left Yesenda wondering what caused him to leave so abruptly. Eventually, she just shook her head and said, "Bards."

Bram's Study

IAIN BURST THROUGH the doors of the Keep searching for Bram. He left Yesenda abruptly because he had an urgent need to work out his feelings.

He spotted Bram in the meeting room and walked over pulling up a chair.

"Iain? What brings you here?"

"Cousin, how did you ken Sorcha was the one for you?"

Bram stared at him a while, trying to read his mood, then said, "I just did. The moment I saw her standing in the snow pointing that bow and arrow at me, I kenned it."

"But how?"

"It was like everything faded away and it was just the two of us who existed in the entire world. As if time stood still and nothing else mattered. It has been that way ever since. She enters a room I feel her there. When she is not around, I crave her company. When I'm with her, I want more of her. Tis like my heart is incomplete without her. But more than anything, tis her nature and character I love above all else and I ken she feels the same."

"What do you mean?"

"Sorcha protected Henderson bairns even when she was my captive. That woman would willingly sacrifice herself to protect them because tis her nature. She stands by my side as my equal, supports me when I'm right and challenges me if she feels I'm wrong. We can talk about everything and nothing, and I would still think it was the best time spent."

"That sounds like true love."

"Aye, but why do you ask?"

"I've been thinking about getting married."

"No!"

"What do you mean, no?"

"Iain, I have been very patient. I have not wanted to interfere in your life."

"What are you talking about, Bram? You interfere in my life all the time, even when we were bairns."

"All right, so I do, but with your women, I'm mostly silent. But not this time."

"Wait, you dinnae want me to get married?"

"That's correct."

"Why not?"

"Because she is not worthy of you. How many times must I say it?"

"What have you got against, Yesenda?"

"Who?"

"Yesenda?"

"Wait, who are you thinking of marrying?"

"Who do you think I'm thinking of marrying?"

"Bloody hell! Iain, I thought you were thinking of Liosa?"

"No! I'm thinking of making Yesenda my wife."

"Oh. Well, in that case, then aye, marry her if Ruadh approves."

"Just like that? You approve?"

"Aye, I approve."

"But now I'm torn."

"What troubles you?"

"What if I'm wrong? I spent my life loving one woman and now I have powerful feelings for another. Is that not worrisome? What if I do the same to Yesenda? I dinnae want to become unfaithful."

"First you are talking about two very different women here. What attracted you to Liosa? Dinnae include her looks. Tell me what it is about being with her you enjoyed."

Iain thought for a while and paused. He tried to come up with something, then paused again.

"Anything?"

"Wait, I'm thinking about her nature. Well... uh. Oh, bollocks!"

"What did you come up with?"

"She was a great bed partner and whenever I saw her, I felt my heart rise."

Bram asked, "Your heart or just your cock? Never mind. Alright, now, let me ask you this. When you're with Yesenda, what do you enjoy?"

Iain instantly smiled when he spoke. "Tis the way she smirks and laughs easily. Tis like sunshine on a blistering wintry day. The way she treats the bairns, giving them the attention they crave. There's a gentleness about her when she is with the bairns."

"What else?"

"Her mind, Bram. She is very smart and insightful. I've never met a more interesting lass. She is quiet observant, and she reads people well. She also bites her bottom lip if she's unsure about something and the way she makes me feel..."

"How does she make you feel?"

"Like I am the most interesting man in the world. When I talk to her about things, she listens intently and hears what I am saying. When I pay her a compliment, she blushes as if she does not ken how bonnie she is."

"If she left and decided never to visit again, what would you do?"

"I would move heaven and earth to find her and drag her back here, then convince her to stay."

"Which brings me to my next question. Every time Liosa left you, why did you not drag her back here?"

"What do you mean?"

"Iain, if a man wants a woman enough, he goes and fetches her. Tis the way of men of our ilk."

"I would never force myself upon a woman unwillingly."

"Of course, I dinnae mean that. If Liosa was the woman for you, nothing should've stopped you from chasing her down and making her see reason."

Iain just raised his brow.

"You can scoff all you like, cousin, but it worked for me when I kidnapped Sorcha."

"Aye, I remember very well. I was there when her kin belted the shit out of you for it."

Bram just ginned and started chuckling.

"You nearly got yourself killed, you daft prick."

"Aye, but lord, it was worth the beating," Bram said, grinning.

"Is there a point to this talk, old married man?"

"The point is, when you love someone with all your heart, nothing will stand in your way. Clearly with Liosa, something always held you back, did it not?" Bram asked with a raised eyebrow.

Iain sighed and nodded.

"Do you ken what that was?"

"A part of me felt like she looked down on all of us all the time. I didna think I could spend my life with someone who would treat my kin, my family that way."

"And with Yesenda?"

"She has a kind soul. I can feel it. It's that powerful."

"And there you have it, Iain. All you need to be certain about, you already ken."

Iain grabbed Bram and gave him an enormous bear hug, then kissed him on the cheek.

"Och, get off me, stupid prick!" Bram grumbled as he tried to wipe his cheek.

"Thank you, cousin," Iain said then he bolted out of the room.

Chapter 9

Friend Zoned

The following day, Yesenda was walking the Keep grounds when Iain appeared. "Yesenda, come with me to the village. It is a nice day for an outing."

Iain grabbed her hand and started walking toward the stables.

"Ah... all right," she said, wondering if she really had a choice.

They travelled by horseback in silence, and Iain remained vigilant. When they arrived, he showed her around the village and took her to places that meant something to him. Iain shared stories of the trouble he and Bram got up to when they were lads. Yesenda enjoyed the outing until their pleasant stroll through the village was interrupted by a most annoying creature.

"Iain!"

Yesenda turned and saw the woman from the hall making her way toward them. She wore a very fine surcoat, and her smile vanished when she saw Yesenda.

"What are you doing here, my love?" she asked Iain.

Iain stiffened, and Yesenda stepped away to give them some privacy. But Iain clasped the back of her kirtle and pulled her back. Yesenda glared at Iain, but he ignored her. She saw anger in the woman.

"I dinnae believe we have met before? I am Iain's woman and who are you?" the woman snapped.

"Liosa," Iain growled in warning. "You are not my woman."

"Iain can deny it all he wants, but I've been sharing his bed for many years," she said to Yesenda.

"That's enough," Iain hissed.

Yesenda felt as if she had walked headfirst into a lover's quarrel. "Mayhap you two should talk while I look at some vendor stalls." She tried to step away, but Iain pulled her back again.

Liosa's eyes narrowed, and she glared at Yesenda.

"What are you doing here, Liosa? I thought you did not like shopping in such a backwater village."

"Well, I changed my mind, Iain. I was thinking of the ring you wanted to buy me. It is still there. Do you remember it?"

"Aye, I remember the ring. You said it was too small and cheap for your liking."

Iain pulled Yesenda even closer and placed his arm around her waist.

"For god's sake, Iain would you stop fondling the woman in front of me? You should be ashamed courting me then cavorting with the likes of her."

Yesenda took a deep breath and decided she was done with whatever this was.

"Cease talking!" she demanded. Giving Liosa a stern look.

Liosa shut her mouth.

"First, Liosa is it? I am a guest of the Henderson laird. Iain has been kind enough to escort me to this fine village. That is all you need to ken about me. Now you may wonder why Iain keeps fondling me when I am trying to give you both privacy, but I can only guess it is to shield himself from you. I just met you and I can say with every intention to insult you, you are vile! If anyone is causing you embarrassment, that would be yourself."

Liosa gasped in outrage and said, "How dare you?"

"Oh, I dare!" Yesenda hissed, then walked away.

Meanwhile, Iain tried to stifle a laugh, then started coughing.

"Iain, I dinnae like that woman. I insist you leave her here and escort me back to the cottage," Liosa said.

"I cannot do that. She is my responsibility."

"And what about me?"

"You are welcome to wait until we have finished our errands."

"Forget it!" Liosa huffed and walked away.

The moment she was gone, Iain turned and ran to catchup with Yesenda.

"I am truly sorry about that."

"'Tis alright Iain, it is none of my concern."

"But it is your concern, seeing as we are friends."

Yesenda did not like being categorized as a friend while that vulgar Liosa woman was his lover. It was a timely reminder that while her feelings for Iain were growing, he only saw her as a *friend*. She frowned.

"You're angry with me?" Iain asked.

"No. It matters not what I feel about you."

"Dinnae say that. It matters. We are close friends and how you feel about me matters."

Yesenda wanted to scream and hit him over the head with a tree branch, but didn't. She just gave him a slight smile and tried to contain her jealously. "Aye, we are friends Iain."

"I enjoy being with you, Yesenda. Our talks have been a great boon to me."

Yesenda sighed and said, "Then I am glad. You have a become a good friend to me too."

More than Friends

THAT NIGHT YESENDA tossed and turned as the noises of the Keep kept her awake. The abbey was a quiet place. Highly organized into routine, whereas Keeps were a completely different beast altogether. After two nights of it, she longed to find a quiet space to rest.

Early the next morning, she slipped out of the Keep for a quiet walk and to find something to occupy her idle hands. She came across Iain's sister, Tyra. Tyra was the clan healer, and she had a healer's cottage in the glen where she treated her patients.

Being raised by nuns, Yesenda knew a fair amount of healing remedies, so before she knew it, she was busily employed assisting Tyra in the healer's cottage. It was just what she needed.

The healer's cottage in the glen was a white longhouse surrounded by a row of smaller cottages. Tyra told her she and Iain remained in the cottages after Bram and the rest of the family moved to the Keep. The view was breathtaking and Yesenda instantly felt at home. This was just what she needed. Fresh air, a river nearby and some chores to keep her busy.

Tyra offered Yesenda the use of an empty cottage if she did not want to stay at the Keep. The cottage used to be occupied by Willa, Bram's sister. Yesenda accepted on the spot, already looking forward to having some privacy away from the Keep and a change of scenery.

Soon the two women fell into a comfortable working routine. Yesenda used the time to treat patients and extract information through informal conversations. One interesting one was with a young lad.

"What is your name?" she asked.

"I'm Seamus."

"Well hello Seamus, now what happened to you?"

"I cut my arm." He held out his arm so she could examine the large cut.

"Oh no. How did you do that?" Yesenda asked.

"I was hiding in a tree, and I fell out of it."

Yesenda began treating the cut, and she kept up the conversation to keep him distracted from the pain.

"Why on earth were you hiding in a tree?"

Seamus lowered his voice and looked about, then leaned close and whispered, "Can you keep a secret?"

Yesenda grinned and said, "Aye, I am a very good keeper of secrets." She continued to apply a poultice and waited.

"I was spying on a man at the blackhouse near the village. Mama says I should not, but I cannot help myself."

"And what did you see?"

"He had a box and gave it to Gordon."

"Who's Gordon?"

"He's my age, and he's the one that's been helping the strangers."

Yesenda's ears pricked up then. "What strangers?"

"The ones that wear the gray robes."

Yesenda froze momentarily and blinked at Seamus. She tied off his bandage then said, "Tell me about them, Seamus."

"I follow them sometimes even though Ma says I should stay put. But I cannot help myself."

"Where do they go?"

"To the old stables."

"What stables?"

"At the Gibson farm."

"Where's that?"

He paused and sighed. "Do you ken nothing about the village?"

Yesenda rolled her eyes and said, "Seamus, I am not from these parts."

"Oh, right. Well, tis beyond the tannery and that's where I saw Gordon leave the box."

"Do you ken what was inside it?"

"Some rolled up paper."

"Seamus, promise me you will stay away from these men. They could be dangerous."

"But... I cannot help myself, tis my nature to be curious."

"What if I agree to watch these men instead and if I see something interesting, I'll tell you? That way you would not get in trouble from your ma."

"Aye, that could work."

Yesenda filed away the information and planned to checkout this blackhouse and the Gibson farm as soon as she could lose the guardsmen.

It was sometime later. Yesenda was mixing a poultice when Lachlan entered the cottage. He frowned, then yelled, "She's in here!" to someone outside. Before Yesenda could ask who he was talking to, the enormous form of Iain Henderson filled the doorway.

Yesenda was about to call a greeting, but paused when she saw Iain's stormy expression. He was furious and his anger was directed at her. Iain stepped over the threshold and moved so fast. One moment he was at the door, the next he was towering over her. She dropped the mortar and pestle and shuffled backwards until her back came up against the wall.

Iain followed suit and placed both hands against the wall on either side of her shoulders. Effectively caging her in. He was breathing heavily, as if trying to rein in his temper before speaking.

"What did I tell you about not leaving the Keep without me?" he growled.

"I am sorry. I saw Tyra and decided to help. I didna mean to—"

Iain did not wait for her to finish her response. Instead, he firmly clasped Yesenda's hand and started walking back toward the door.

"What are you doing?" Yesenda protested.

"I am taking you back to the Keep!" he snapped and continued to pull her behind him.

There were no words to describe what Iain felt in that moment other than livid. He'd gone to the Keep early to see if Yesenda needed an escort, only to discover her missing. He and his men scoured the Keep and surrounding area. As more time passed with no word of her whereabouts, Iain felt genuine fear for her safety. The thought of something terrible happening to Yesenda, especially with a stranger searching for her, created a fierce need within Iain to protect her. Suffice to say, he was besieged with worry.

So, when he entered the cottage to find her messing about with herbal pastes as if she did not have a care in the world, his brain imploded. He knew he was being completely unreasonable, but all he wanted to do was wrap her in soft wool and tie her to his bed to keep her out of harm's way.

Tyra yelled, "Iain, stop! I told Yesenda she can help me and stay in Willa's cottage while she's here."

Damn it to hell! Iain remembered he had told no one Liosa was staying in that cottage.

He also did not want Yesenda to think there was anything between him and Liosa.

Iain was at a crisis point. He realized at that moment that he had to decide between Liosa, who represented his past, or Yesenda, who symbolized the future.

"Yesenda cannot stay there. Tis already occupied," he said and glared at Tyra.

Once it dawned on Tyra what Iain meant, she shouted, "You get Liosa out of there!"

"Liosa needs to remain there until I can make *other* arrangements." When Iain spoke those words out loud, he knew right down to his soul that he was letting go of the past and embracing the future with both hands. He was going to see that Liosa left and never darkened his doorstep again.

Yesenda glanced between the two siblings in confusion when Liosa entered the cottage. Then she realized Iain had moved his lover into Willa's cottage.

Yesenda tried to pull her hand out of Iain's, but the big brute tightened his grip and refused to let go. If the situation was not already awkward, she would have kicked him in the shin, but there was an underlying tension thrumming through the longhouse and Yesenda decided it was best not to add more turmoil to the situation.

"Iain? Are you taking me to the markets today? You promised," Liosa said.

"It will have to wait. I need to take someone back to the Keep," Iain replied.

Liosa glanced at Iain, and Yesenda's joined hands, and her eyes flashed with anger.

"Then I shall come with you too," Liosa said. She marched toward the two of them and separated their hands, then dragged Iain out of the cottage, no doubt to have words.

Iain relented, but before he left, he paused, turned briefly, and gave Yesenda a piercing glance. "Dinnae go anywhere without me again."

Yesenda just frowned, overcome with something akin to jealousy. Then she mentally slapped herself. Iain was not and would never be hers. She walked back to the table and resumed making a paste. She resolved to erase any fanciful thoughts about Iain bloody Henderson.

After the morning's drama, the rest of the day went without incident. Yesenda spent the afternoon helping the Henderson women, Tyra, Willa and Fia, prepare supper while they enjoyed a dram of whiskey. They sat around the table in the longhouse preparing vegetables as they shared the local news. In that time, Yesenda learned everything she needed to know about Iain and Liosa's relationship.

"Liosa Haxton comes and goes as she pleases. She was Iain's first love, and they were together for a time. Then she causes trouble, and they part ways. She returns when she hears Iain might lose interest, then she's gone again," Tyra said.

Willa just nodded and poured herself another cup of whiskey.

"Like the time Iain courted a bonnie lass from Glasgow. Liosa got wind of it and reappeared long enough to stake her claim, then she was gone again. Tis the same pattern over and over," Fia said as she shelled peas.

"We dinnae like her for Iain. He deserves far better," Willa grumbled.

"Where does she go after they part ways?" Yesenda asked.

"That's the troubling thing. We dinnae ken, but we believe there is a wealthy merchant somewhere. One does not wear her fine garments without a steady supply of coin. Iain has begged for her hand in marriage many times, but she refuses," Tyra said.

"She does not want him, but she cannot bear for him to find someone else, so she refuses to let go," Yesenda said.

"Aye, you have the right of it," Fia agreed.

Yesenda kept her eye on her task and sighed inwardly. She knew then any feelings she had for Iain would never be returned. While he might act protective around her, she was merely a duty to him. Liosa was the woman he chose repeatedly.

Yesenda decided life was too short to pine for a man who loved another. At that moment, she released her fanciful crush and was determined to keep her distance from now on.

Scorn

LIOSA FOLLOWED IAIN out of the cottage, then gave him a blistering earful as he continued to walk her to the markets.

"Why were you holding that woman's hand? Who is she?" Liosa demanded.

"She's our guest. I am charged with the duty of guarding her."

"Find someone else to guard her, Iain."

"I agreed to it. She needs to be kept out of harm's way."

"Do you have to hold her hand in order to keep her safe?"

Iain said nothing, but kept walking.

"Slow down! I cannot keep up."

He slowed and waited for her to catch up to him. When she did, she tried to take his hand, but he shook hers away.

"Iain! Hold my hand, damn you."

"Why? We are not together, Liosa. I ken you have family problems and need to remain here, but I think tis time you returned home. I'll escort you to the markets, but tomorrow you will return to your home."

She looked as if he'd slapped her.

"Dinnae look at me like that. I've told you; there is no longer anything between us. You dinnae want to marry or settle down, so what is the point? Besides, I have duties to see to and I cannot be escorting you about the place."

"Oh, but you're willing to take that whore everywhere!"

"She is not a whore! She is a sweet lass who has spent most of her life in an abbey. Dinnae be so disrespectful."

"Wait... she was in an abbey all this time?"

"Aye."

Liosa glanced at the longhouse for a moment and then continued walking. She was deep in thought.

Iain preferred it that way.

When she spoke again, he was rather stunned.

"Iain, let's get married."

"What?"

"You've asked me before and I've decided to accept."

"Well, I withdraw my request."

"But you just said—"

"Tis too late Liosa. Please understand, I no longer want to marry you."

"But all these years you've pursued me and suddenly she arrives and you dinnae want me anymore?"

"No, all these years I was a fool, and it took that lass in there to make me realize it."

"Iain, I am the love of your life. You told me so yourself. You will tire of this woman and then you'll be sorry you treated me so terribly."

"Liosa, are you jealous of her?"

"Of course I am! She is trying to steal you away from me."

Iain muttered, "She doesna have to try hard."

"Iain, you ken I will always love you."

He just rolled his eyes and kept walking.

"'Tis true! I am just confused, and I just need time to—"

"That's the problem, Liosa. Everything is always about your needs and your wants and your plans. I am done with it all."

"Iain, please, let us start afresh—"

"You dinnae understand, Liosa. What I am telling you is that I no longer want to be with you. For the first time in my life, I realize I deserve better. I suggest when we return, you pack your things and go home."

"But I have nowhere else to go." She looked forlorn.

"Liosa, stop with the games. I will not stomach it anymore. Go back to the men who pay you to have the life you want."

"Fine then. You need not escort me back. I shall remain in the village. I still have friends there, but mark my words, Iain Henderson, you'll be sorry you ever threw me over for someone else."

Iain just shook his head, wondering not for the first time what he ever saw in Liosa.

Breakfast

IAIN ROSE EARLY THE next morning. He made his way to the longhouse to prepare breakfast before it became overrun with Tyra's patrons. When he opened the door, he was greeted with a glimpse of his future.

Yesenda was barefoot in a plain kirtle. Her hair was braided and secured into a bun while she pulled out freshly baked bread from the wood-fire oven. The heat gave a slight flush to her cheeks. Some tendrils had come loose from the bun. When she turned towards him, she blushed, and it floored him with the vision she made first thing in the morning. *Bonnie.* The second thing to assail him was the delicious aromas of her cooking.

Iain had to take a breath and remind himself to calm down as his heart raced at the overwhelming vision she created.

Then she smiled. It was genuine and warm and welcoming.

"Morning, Iain. Come join me if you will. I've made food to break our fast. Tyra has gone to the Keep but will return later."

Iain stared slightly, mouth ajar, at the table. There was a pitcher of fresh milk and churned butter. A platter of oat cakes and honey, strips of fried pork and eggs. Some fruit and cheese and Yesenda had just placed the freshly baked bread on a board. She was slicing pieces and spreading butter on them. He licked his lips and his stomach grumbled. He was hungry in more ways than one, and it was not just for food. It was for this. *All of this.*

"The food smells delicious, lass. You must have been up early."

"In the abbey, we wake very early for prayers and to do our chores. Tis just a habit, I suppose."

She finished buttering the bread, then paused and asked, "Is Liosa going to join us? There is plenty of food."

Iain shook his head and said, "Liosa left last night. She will *not* be returning, Yesenda." He held her gaze as if he was trying to relay some pertinent news.

Yesenda felt elated with the news, but she reminded herself this was just their way. Liosa would return eventually, as she always did, and Iain would take her back. She cleared her throat and said, "Oh, I see. Um... I have made an herbal brew if you would like a warm drink. It was especially cool this morn."

Iain looked about the main room. There was a pot boiling over the fire.

"Who lit the fire?" he asked.

"I did."

He blinked at her for a while with a confused expression.

"Tis not hard to light a fire, Iain. Anyone can do it."

Iain noticed the wood also piled neatly on the side. He had planned to fill the wood basket that morning.

"Who cut the wood for you?"

"I did. The basket was empty, but I found the wood pile and axe out the back."

Iain just paused and kept staring at her. Then he noticed she took on a worried expression.

"Have I done something wrong? Am I not supposed to use the wood from the back?" She paused and bit her lip; afraid she might have overstepped somehow.

"No... no, not at all, lass. Tis just a surprise is all. I... normally do everything myself if it's just me and Lios..." His voice tapered off because Iain did not want to finish that line.

Yesenda visibly relaxed. "Oh well, today you can rest, Iain. Please come and sit. This is your family home, after all."

Iain moved towards the table and said, "Love, the food looks delicious, and I am famished."

Yesenda beamed then and started fussing over him. She went to get the pot of tea from the fireplace, but Iain got up and took the iron rods off her. "Here, let me do it." Their hands touched as he took the tools from her, and they stood close to each other. Yesenda blushed, feeling a thousand lightning bolts go through her with the feel of his skin. Iain took a sharp intake of breath, then Yesenda quickly stepped back and hurried back to the table.

They sat beside one another. Iain noted how well they worked together. Yesenda added more spices to the warm brew and let it steep, whilst Iain served the food onto their trenchers. Yesenda then moved to the oatcakes and drizzled honey syrup on them. She placed them in a side bowl for Iain while he placed pieces of meat on her slice of bread as she poured warm brew into two cups. Iain did not need to ask for a thing because Yesenda saw to it.

He had never known a meal to be this easy.

They said a quick word of thanks for the bounty and then dug in with gusto.

Iain groaned when he bit into the fresh bread and butter and savored the taste.

"Damn, woman, what is in this butter?" he asked.

Yesenda grinned. "I added some salt and sage to give it flavor."

He devoured the eggs and groaned at the delicious taste.

"Here, eat them with some of this mashed potato." Yesenda dished up a fluffy spoonful and heaped some on the side of his trencher.

Iain grinned and dug in, then groaned some more when the mash melted in his mouth. Yesenda loved the way he openly showed his appreciation.

"Yesenda," he said, while chewing another mouthful. "This is the best breakfast I've ever eaten in my life. What did you do with the pork?"

"Oh, I just fried it with wild onion, garlic, and tomatoes."

"And the potatoes?"

"'Tis just mashed with a wee bit of milk and butter."

"You need to teach Cook how to prepare meals like this."

Yesenda beamed with pride every time Iain groaned with delight at the food. It was satisfying cooking for someone who clearly enjoyed it.

"What are your plans for today, love?" he asked. "I have some clan matters, but I can escort you later, wherever you need to go."

"Oh, I am not planning on much today, Iain. I will probably remain here and help Tyra when she returns from the weaving circle."

"Aye, that sounds like a safe option. I'll send Kieran here just in case."

Yesenda nodded. She did not like lying to Iain, but by the same token, she needed to see about the blackhouse and this Gibson farm. She had met Kieran previously, and he seemed an easy-going type, so she agreed. Little did she know it was going to land her in even more hot water.

Chapter 10

The Search

"Yesenda, this is not part of the plan," Kieran, her guardsman, mumbled.

"Kieran, tis perfectly safe, it's only the village and what could possibly happen to me here?"

"Trust me, I've been guarding troublesome women for many years, and something always happens."

"Are you calling me troublesome? I lead a very quiet life Kieran; I am no trouble at all."

"You dinnae fool me, lass. Tis always the quiet ones who will get you killed."

Yesenda burst out laughing and just shook her head. "Kieran, you are far too suspicious for your own good."

"See this?" Kieran asked. He lowered his leine to reveal a scar on the back of his shoulder.

"Aye."

"That was from a knife wound inflicted while guarding Amelia MacGregor. At the time we all thought her 'quiet'. Well, she turned out to be the most troublesome woman in the whole of Scotland. I dinnae ken how Beiste puts up with her, to be honest."

Yesenda grinned. She'd met Amelia and could attest the woman was anything but quiet.

"I can assure you Kieran, nothing will happen. Besides, if there's any danger, I will protect you."

"You will protect me?" He looked outraged. "You will do no such thing! If there's danger, you will hide, you daft woman. That comment right there has me on my guard."

"Oh look, here we are," Yesenda exclaimed so she could change the subject. They'd reached the village and Yesenda pointed towards an inn. "Can we get some refreshments there? I'm parched."

"Aye, I suppose we can do that. But we'll not stay too long. This time of day it gets crowded."

Yesenda was counting on it. The blackhouse young Seamus told her about was behind the inn and a crowd was the prefect distraction.

Once inside, they ordered, and when the mead arrived, Yesenda excused herself to visit the garderobe. Kieran deemed it safe, seeing as the separate building, although a slight distance away, was still within view of the inn.

Yesenda walked down the thoroughfare and as she passed a serving woman, she slipped a coin into her palm and said, "Keep smiling and pretend we ken each other."

The serving woman did as she asked. Then Yesenda said, "I'll give you two more if you keep this between us and if you can distract my companion over there."

"The braw handsome man you came in with?" the serving woman asked.

"Aye."

The woman clasped the coins and said, "Twould be my pleasure. And dinnae worry, your secret is safe with me." She winked and meandered her way over to Kieran.

Yesenda glanced back to see Kieran distracted. She sprinted out the back alleyway.

The Blackhouse, Glencoe Village

LIOSA MADE HER WAY to the usual meeting point. Her lover was back in the burgh, and her patron paid her handsomely to ensure he was entertained. It was the only reason Liosa returned to *Glencoe* so often. She had a love hate relationship with things from her past and that included Iain. He represented a time when life was simpler, and she had not fallen into a world of depravity. Liosa sought Iain's goodness when the darkness threatened to overwhelm her, but she also despised him for it because it was a stark contrast to the life she had chosen. In the end, she just made them both miserable. But seeing Iain moving on with someone else was too much to bear. Fortunately, the woman he was courting was the same one her lover was searching for, so Liosa felt no guilt at doing what she was about to do.

"I've found her," Liosa said.

The pilgrim asked, "Where?"

"She is a guest of the Hendersons. She lives in the Keep, but they have her guarded. The description matches except her hair is now a sandy blonde colour. She recently left an abbey where she lived since a bairn."

"Then I will send my brothers for her. You risk a lot by coming to see me in the open," he said.

"I could not bear to stay away. I hope I have served you well with this information."

"We shall see. Now go." He dismissed her with a wave of his hand.

"You wish me to leave?" she asked, surprised.

"*Oui.*"

"But I thought mayhap you might want some company tonight. It has been a long time, and I returned to *Glencoe* once I received your missive."

He raised a brow and asked, "Have you abstained from relations with other men?"

"Aye, I have. I have kept myself for you."

"Well, seeing as you're here, I suppose you may as well earn your keep. Take off your garments and lie on the bed. Ready yourself for me, Liosa."

Liosa grinned, walked towards the bed, and slowly stripped down. Then she seductively climbed up onto it and lay on her back. She held the bed head and spread her thighs.

The pilgrim eyed her lazily, then stared into the fire. Having recently bathed, he wore only a loincloth. After a long time contemplating his next move, he was interrupted.

Liosa said, "Are you going to stand there all night, my liege? It is far more pleasurable over here."

He gazed at the sultry woman on his bed, and his eyelids hooded with lust. He decided Miriam Ferguson could wait a little longer. For now, he would partake of Liosa's ample charms and use her body well. She had been his lover for years, and they paid handsomely for her services.

The pilgrim removed the cloth he wore about his waist and strolled towards her. He saw her eyes glaze over with lust when she viewed his naked form. The pilgrim took care of his body and his appearance because people were superficial creatures. Wealth, privilege, and beauty were powerful influencers, and he used all three to maximum advantage.

Liosa licked her lips when she viewed his enormous cock and the piercings at the tip. He grinned and thought she was a whore to her very core. She claimed she slept with no others, but the pilgrim was skeptical. He knew Liosa would do anything for money, even betray her own kin. She was outwardly charming with a corrupted soul. Just like him.

As he raked her body with his striking blue eyes, he subconsciously rubbed the spot on his arm that bore the tattoo of a war club. It was an emblem of the monastic order he was born into. An order his twin brother established and one he was going to claim for his self. *The*

Brotherhood. They dressed alike so no one could tell who led and who followed, but the pilgrim's reign of terror was only just beginning. He doubted Liosa would come near him if she knew his true nature.

"Patience *mademoiselle*," he said. "I am coming."

YESENDA WAS CROUCHED low behind a tall hedgerow. She moved closer trying to get a look at the people within. Inside was a woman spread naked on the bed and a naked man standing by the fireplace. She could not see clearly but the woman's garments, which were thrown over a chair, looked familiar.

Liosa? she thought to herself.

It didn't take a scholar to figure out what was happening between the two people inside. Yesenda was tossing up whether to wait longer or just barge in there when she was startled by a noise beside her.

"What's happening inside? I cannot, see?" a young boy whispered beside her.

"Seamus! Did I not tell you to stay away?"

Yesenda dragged Seamus away from the window and shuffled him out of view.

"I was curious. Tis in my nature, remember?"

"Well, you need to take care that your curious nature doesna get you killed. Your ma is right. You should not be sneaking about, peeking through windows."

"But you're doing it."

"That's different. I'm a grown woman."

When Yesenda glanced back at the house, she could hear moaning coming from within. *Damn!* She needed to get Seamus back to his mother and then hie back to the inn.

They were startled when Kieran asked, "Is there a reason you two are hiding in the bushes?" He was standing by the road with his arms folded across his chest and glaring at Yesenda.

Yesenda quickly grabbed Seamus and stood to the side. "Um... I saw this young lad, and I wanted to make sure his arm was healing properly. I was about to go find his ma. Isn't that right Seamus?"

"Aye," Seamus said as he shook his head to indicate 'no'.

Yesenda nudged him, and he started nodding.

"Well, we best go find his ma then," Kieran said, giving them a skeptical look.

When they were walking back to the glen, Kieran asked, "What were you really doing in the bushes, Yesenda?"

"Exactly what I told you," she replied.

He sighed. "So, it's going to be like that, is it?"

"Like what? Kieran, I told you, I found the lad wandering about and agreed to help him."

Kieran just shook his head and sighed. When they reached the healer's cottage, he escorted her inside and closed the door. He then stood outside by the window.

Several moments passed before Kieran yelled, "Yesenda?"

"Aye?" she responded and came to the window.

"The next time you pay someone to distract me, make sure tis not Margarite. That woman cannot keep a secret if her life depended on it."

Yesenda blushed with embarrassment then said, "Kieran... I—"

But he was already walking away. Then she heard him yell, "No trouble? My arse!"

It was dusk, Yesenda was in the cottage when the door was flung open, and Iain came stalking in. Again, staring directly at her, and he was furious.

"Why were you in the village today?" he growled.

"I wanted to—."

"Dinnae trifle with me, Yesenda. Kieran told me you snuck off. Why?" He moved closer and stared down at her.

Yesenda gave a half truth. "I... wanted to find out who the stranger was in the village. That is all. I was just curious."

Iain's eyes flashed with concern, then he said, "Leave it to us. Bram has men keeping a lookout and Yesenda, I will protect you."

The way his eyes softened as they roamed over her face mesmerized Yesenda.

Iain had moved even closer now, and he leaned in slightly, closing his eyes momentarily. When he opened them again, he said, "Gods, you're a bonnie lass. I cannot seem to stay away."

Yesenda was finding it harder to breathe with Iain in such proximity. His lips were mere inches away from hers. Then she felt his hands on her waist as he gently pulled her into his arms. Their bodies touching, their breathing erratic. Yesenda breathed in his woodsy masculine scent and made a whimpering sound when he lowered his head and placed a chaste kiss on her neck. Her body was on fire as Iain's hands continued to caress her back. She'd never felt this way about any man before. Being with Iain this past week made her feel emotions she had never experienced.

Iain softly whispered in her ear as he nuzzled her neck, "I would die before I let any harm come to you, Yesenda. Dinnae risk your safety running about the village inviting trouble."

"I will try not to do it again," she replied, rubbing her cheek against his.

He raised his head and stared at her with a raised eyebrow. "You will not do it again. There is no *'try'* about it.

"All right," she whispered.

They stood for a moment in silence.

"Iain, mayhap you should let me go now."

"No. I dinnae want to."

"Why not?"

"Because you belong to me."

It was Yesenda's turn to raise her eyebrow. "I do?"

"Aye. I have decreed it." He grinned.

Yesenda smirked. "That is very high handed of you."

"Would you welcome my hands on you, Yesenda?" he said seductively.

"Aye, Iain, I would."

"And would you welcome my lips on yours?"

She nodded. Then Yesenda wound her arms about his neck and stood on tiptoe. "I would very much like to taste your lips, Iain," she rasped.

Iain was undone. He did not hesitate and within seconds; he claimed her lips with his own and groaned when she burrowed in closer. Iain laid siege to her mouth and tongue, and Yesenda matched his fervor.

Iain felt only bliss and a deep need to be inside her. To claim her in all ways that mattered and make her his. The scent of wildflowers invaded his senses, and he saw no one and nothing else other than Yesenda. His present and his future. *Just his.*

Yesenda was panting in gasps as Iain's hands continued to caress and coax the passion within her.

She made a startled sound when Iain grasped her backside and lifted her so she straddled his waist and she held onto his shoulders. Iain then walked her over to the table and sat her atop it. Their lips still fused together; their bodies entwined.

Yesenda began her own exploration. Running her hands across his arms and across his chest. Savoring the feel of his muscular physique. She was beyond aroused. She felt positively wicked.

Iain kissed a trail down her neck, then his lips moved lower. He gently pushed her backward until her back was on the table, and Iain was hovering above her, his hips in line with the juncture between her leg.

Yesenda could feel his arousal through the material and her body erupted in goose bumps.

"Do you want me, lass?"

"Aye, Iain, I want you. I shouldn't, but I do."

Iain kissed her then and began lifting the hem of her gown, caressing her bare skin with his hands.

His eyes were clouded with lust as he continued to drink in the sight of her, laid out before him like a veritable feast. Iain suddenly came to his senses when the rest of the room intruded into his vision. He saw Yesenda in all her radiance offering herself to him... on a table in the longhouse where anyone could walk in on them.

He shook his head to clear the lust fog. He could not do that to her. If she was innocent, he did not want her first time to be on a bloody table.

"Iain? Is everything all right?" she asked, worry marred her features.

Iain stood completely still. His breathing was ragged. "I cannot do this. Not with you." He quickly pulled down her gown and stepped away from her.

The flames of her passion were doused in that moment. Iain looked positively disgusted, and she suddenly felt embarrassed. He must think her a wanton woman with no scruples.

She quickly sat up in horror, realizing how close they'd come to coupling on the family dining table. It mortified her she had been tempted. Then she remembered. Iain was deeply in love with Liosa and would be for life.

"I... I'm sorry," she rasped. She gently shoved Iain out of her way and jumped down.

"Yesenda, wait. I'm sorry lass, tis just that—"

"No, tis not your fault. I did not mean for it to go so far. I... I have never done that before and... I ken I am not her." Yesenda had already turned away and was straightening her dress.

"What do you mean?" Iain looked confused. "Yesenda, tis not you, tis just that—"

Before he could finish his line, the door burst opened, and a guardsman entered.

"Iain, you're needed at the Keep. Mistress Sorcha has gone into labor. The laird needs you."

Iain glanced at Yesenda. He had so much he wanted to say, but instead he turned and headed for the door.

"Wait!" Yesenda called out. "I'm coming. They might need my help."

Iain nodded. "Aye, tis a good idea." He clasped her hand in his, then both ran out of the cottage together.

Despite the earlier disaster of their *almost* coupling, Iain and Yesenda remained inseparable throughout the ordeal. Yesenda was not sure why, but anytime Iain was near her, he would reach for her hand and clasp it. Or he would physically pull her close, so she sat beside him.

When the danger to Sorcha and the new babe was over, Yesenda wept tears of joy wrapped in Iain's arms. She savored the moment because she knew it could not last.

She was right.

Avoidance

YESENDA WAS AVOIDING him. Iain knew it right down to his bones. Every time they were in the same room together, she would make some excuse and leave. Even worse, he would wake early to join her for breakfast and all he would find was a plate warming by the hearth. Her thoughtfulness touched him, but he also wanted to break her neck for denying him her company. Iain missed her plain and simple. But Yesenda was adept at avoidance. He could not get a single moment alone with her. And lord did he want some alone time to talk about 'the table' incident.

Finally, an opportunity arose. The MacGregors were returning to *Glenorchy,* now that Sorcha's lying-in was over. While the women were doing their long round of farewells, he spied Yesenda standing aside, giving them privacy.

Iain made his way over and just stood beside her.

Yesenda *felt* him before she saw him.

"It will be a lot quieter once the MacGregors leave," Iain said.

"Aye. I will miss the bairns. They are a handful, though," Yesenda replied.

"That they are, but they're good natured. Although I'll not miss all the shouting."

Yesenda looked confused and said, "I did not hear the bairns shouting overmuch."

"I was referring to their parents."

Yesenda chuckled at Iain's quip. "Tis true. Although it was mostly the men doing the bellowing."

"That's because their women were so infuriating it caused them to bellow."

They both grinned.

Iain cleared his throat and said, "Yesenda, I was hoping to talk to you about what happened that night at the cottage. I—"

"Tis fine, Iain. I understand."

"Understand what?"

"I understand why you dinnae want me and tis all right. You are in love with Liosa. It was not right for us to do what we were about to do."

"What do you mean I dinnae want you?"

"Iain, you looked at me as if I were a sea monster. I meant what I said. I ken your heart will always belong to someone else. You were right to stop things before they went too far."

"You think I am still in love with Liosa?" Iain had to take a step back, stunned by the revelation.

"Can we not talk about this anymore? Oh look, I think someone is calling me." Yesenda had taken one step when Iain hauled her back.

"I dinnae ken what you've heard about me and Liosa but I can assure you, she has no place in my life or my heart. I ended it with her before you arrived. No matter what foolish idea you have in your head, ken this, I desire you with every part of my being."

"Then why did you stop?"

"Because I want our first time together to be more than a quick swive on a table. You deserve better than that."

"Oh," Yesenda said, seeing things from a different perspective.

"If you will allow it, I would like to court you properly," Iain said.

Yesenda took a sharp intake of breath. "You want to court me?" she asked.

"Aye, I want us to ken each other better because I enjoy being with you."

That filled Yesenda with elation that Iain had feelings for her as well. But despair followed that elation when she remembered Edmund and the *Order* and all the secrets she kept.

Iain wanted to court this version of her. This was all a *facade*. There was no way she could give him a future when hers was so uncertain.

"What say you, Yesenda? Mayhap we can spend more time together and see how we get on."

"Iain, I am sorry, but I dinnae think I can. I will leave soon."

"When?" he demanded.

"When Ruadh comes for me. I have other matters to attend to."

"Ruadh will not return for a while yet. It will give us ample time to ken one another better."

"You dinnae understand, Iain. There is much you dinnae ken about me. And you will not like it—"

"Just consider it, Yesenda." He leaned down and brushed a quick kiss across her lips. Then walked away.

As Iain walked away, he vowed that he would win her over. No matter her objections, he knew in his heart that she would play a role in his future. He hoped by the time Ruadh returned, there would be no need for Yesenda to leave.

Chapter 11

The Gibson Farm

A missive arrived for Yesenda. It was a note from Edmund's foster parents, Sienna, and Gideon. They had settled in *Kentallen*. They were still waiting on word from Brother Mateo, but in the meantime, they were safe. Edmund was safe. Yesenda decided she would join them soon to make sure he remained that way.

After the MacGregors left the Keep, things seemed to settle into a normal routine, allowing her ample time to herself. She discovered a simple method to avoid Iain. Yesenda told Tyra she was going to see Sorcha, then she told Willa she was with Fia and so forth. Each woman assumed she was with the other, so when Iain asked of her whereabouts, she was always accounted for within the Keep. In the meantime, Yesenda was free to explore.

And so it was Yesenda found herself at the abandoned Gibson farm. Dressed in trews and a tunic with her black hooded cloak, she remained hidden. She was waiting patiently for one particular person. *Gordon.*

He left the parchments, then rode off. Just as Seamus said he would.

Yesenda waited patiently until Gordon was out of view, then she slipped inside the stable. She looked for likely places one could hide a missive. Then she saw it. There was a section where the hay was disturbed. She walked towards it and brushed it aside and sure enough, there was a small box under it.

She reached inside and pulled out the parchment. It had a strange wax seal on it with the letter 'M.' The message was in Latin. It translated to, *"Brother S — Find Miriam Ferguson and Kill her. Long live the Brotherhood."* The message then described her appearance.

Yesenda knew about the *Brotherhood*. Even if she destroyed this letter, they would no doubt already be on their way to Henderson Land.

Yesenda resealed the missive with a blank piece of parchment and destroyed the original.

Then she bolted for her horse. She needed to get to Henderson Keep. Her greatest fear had been realized. She had brought danger directly to innocent people.

The Brotherhood

YESENDA SLIPPED BACK into the Keep and became a shadow, making her way through the dimly lit passageways, scanning her surroundings for any threat of danger. The rest of the Keep moved about, oblivious to the deadly threat headed their way.

The men were in the training grounds, the women in the weaving rooms. She climbed up to the turret and scanned the area, trying to spot any anomalies.

While she was patrolling the upper floor, she heard several noises coming from the drawing room. The whimper of a small child and Sorcha's voice speaking in a panic tone. Then a voice cut through them all. It was a *Norman/French* accent.

Yesenda tiptoed to the staircase, then she removed her shoes and climbed the corner of the wall. She rested one foot on one side and the other foot on the opposite side and used her vantage point to look inside the room. Perched high above, she could see what was happening inside the room whilst remaining hidden. Her blood ran cold. For inside was a gray monk.

"Where is Miriam Ferguson?" he asked Sorcha.

"I dinnae ken who that is? Please dinnae hurt the bairns," Sorcha pleaded.

Sorcha had her hands bound behind her back and little Mysie was carrying baby Cináed in her arms. The monk held a war club above Mysie's head, threatening to end her life.

Yesenda decided enough was enough. She needed to end this swiftly and protect them all. She was about to move, but cursed when she saw Iain clambering up the stairs. He was going to ruin everything. There was no way she could hide the truth from Iain now. She only hoped he would not look upon her with revulsion once he discovered her true nature.

"Iain!" she whispered.

He looked about in confusion.

"Up here," she said.

Yesenda would never forget the shocked expression on Iain's face when he gazed upward and saw her perched in the corner. If the situation was not dire, she would have burst out laughing. She knew the way she balanced against the wall with one hand and two bare feet, was most likely something he'd never seen before.

She signaled for him to remain quiet, then with hand gestures and mouthed words she made him understand there was danger up ahead and he was to stay put. But Iain did not care to listen because he withdrew his claymore and quietly moved to the doorway of the drawing room.

Yesenda just rolled her eyes and shook her head. *Men!*

She knew she had minutes at the most before the monk killed everyone in that room. That was the nature of the brotherhood. They threatened once, then followed through. She sighed and then quietly hoisted herself up onto the rafters and made her way via the ceiling into the drawing room. Yesenda waited until everything was in place, then silently climbed down and waited in the alcove's shadow.

"You will tell me where Miriam Ferguson is, or I will kill the girl."

Yesenda heard Sorcha pleading with the monk to let the bairns go. It broke her heart to see little Mysie trembling in fear as she clutched her little cousin. Yesenda knew it was her fault they were in that position. She should never have visited the Hendersons. She clenched her jaw and resolved to end their torment.

Yesenda slowly stepped out of the shadows and said, *"Relinquam illam solam. Ego hic."* – *Leave her alone. I am here.*

The monk replied, *"Miriam, ego expectavimus diu."* – *I have waited a long time.*

Yesenda took a step closer and said, "When did you become such a coward that you would quarrel with bairns? Let them go. I have what you want."

He replied, "You think me foolish? I know what you are. I will not make it past the door unless I have the babe as safe passage."

Yesenda ignored him and calmly addressed Mysie, saying, "Dinnae drop your cousin. Hold him tight."

Mysie sniffled, nodded, and held Cináed a little closer to her chest.

"If you leave the bairns alone, I will come with you unarmed and make sure we both leave in one piece," Yesenda said, hoping to buy some time.

The monk contemplated her offer.

Yesenda could just make out Iain hovering beyond the door. She waited for Iain to do what she assumed he would. Then she could do what she was trained to do.

As the seconds ticked by, Iain finally stepped into the room, and when he did, his shoe hit a creaky floorboard, giving away his position instantly.

That was what Yesenda was waiting for. Men are so predictable, she thought. Then she moved. Yesenda sprinted towards the monk while he was momentarily distracted. She reached under her cloak and pulled out her mace.

"Run, Mysie," she yelled. Mysie ran to Sorcha.

The monk sensed her approach and swung his spiked war club in Yesenda's direction. She pivoted and planted both feet firmly on the floor, then spun her mace upwards, blocking his weapon with equal force.

"Brother Mateo has taught you well," he grunted with a look of admiration. "I underestimated you."

"Most men do."

Then his face took on a grim determination as he swung his war club at her head.

Yesenda expected the move and blocked it.

"You have a strong right hand, but you'll need to do better to kill me," the monk said, laughing.

Yesenda knew he was taunting her, but Brother Mateo had indeed trained her well. As she fought, his words rang clear in her mind. *They strike fast, like vipers. Focus your mind. Anticipate every move.*

The monk was adept at his weapon. So was Yesenda. She blocked hit after hit, expertly spinning her mace in her right hand with Mateo's voice in her head. *Respect the mace, Yesenda. It is an extension of your body. It is only as effective as the one who wields it.*

Iain took a moment to process what he was seeing, as he watched in utter fascination as Yesenda fought the monk. He had always thought her graceful in movement, but nothing prepared him for this. Her moves were fast and fluid. He inhaled a sharp breath. *She was magnificent.* To think he thought she needed protecting.

He shook his head so he could focus, then entered the fray.

Yesenda felt Iain beside her and did not want to think about what he thought of her. She would deal with it later.

"Where the bloody hell did you get that thing?" he growled as he wielded his claymore.

"A lady never tells," Yesenda said. Not taking her eyes off the monk.

"What on earth are they teaching at the abbey nowadays?" Iain muttered as he narrowly missed a blow to the head.

"You'd be surprised," Yesenda replied.

"Get down!" Iain yelled. Yesenda ducked as Iain blocked the club with his claymore.

"Move!" Yesenda shouted, and Iain sidestepped as Yesenda swung her mace at the monk's left side to hinder him.

The monk switched his war club to his left hand and blocked her attack. He chuckled. "That's the problem with right-handed women. You cannot match my skill." He ran at Yesenda so fast. It almost took her by surprise. *Almost.*

The monk aimed his war club at her right hand to dislodge her weapon. In a move he hadn't expected, Yesenda flicked her mace behind her back. All the while, she kept her eyes on him. He watched the mace spin in the air behind her. Then she raised her arm and caught the handle in her left hand. It was an effortless move and he knew he had made a grave error in judgement when she brought the mace crashing down against his unguarded rib. It connected, and he heard the crunching sound as the flanges broke bones and tore through his flesh. He winced in pain as shock registered on his face.

"'Tis lucky that I am left-handed," Yesenda smirked as the monk collapsed to his knees.

He still attempted to swing his club as blood poured from his side. Iain slammed his foot on the handle and kicked it away.

The monk grimaced in pain as blood poured from his wound. His breathing was shallow, and Yesenda was familiar with the sound. It was from broken ribs and a punctured lung. If she did not help him soon, he would die.

"Who sent you?" Yesenda demanded.

He remained silent.

"Tell me who sent you, and I can heal your wounds?" Yesenda said.

Still, he remained silent.

"Answer her!" Iain shouted.

The monk looked up at her, his face a mask of unsettling serenity. He pulled out a dagger and yelled, *"Nam Episcopus et Anglia!"–For the Bishop. For England.* Then he stabbed himself in the heart.

"No!" she yelled, but it was too late.

"Why did he call you Miriam Ferguson?" Iain demanded.

"I dinnae ken, I just played along," she lied. But Yesenda's mind was already alert to more attacks.

As Bram entered the room, he assured her Sorcha, and the bairns were well.

Yesenda warned him the danger had not passed.

"What do you mean?" Bram asked.

"This man is a part of a brotherhood. They travel in twos and wherever they go, people end up dead," she replied.

"What does that mean?" Iain demanded.

"It means we are still in danger until we find his companion." She turned to Sorcha and asked, "Did he mention anything else? Anything out of the ordinary?"

"Aye, he said something about healers."

"Where is Tyra?" she asked.

"She was headed back to the glen," Bram said.

Yesenda did not wait. She bolted out the door.

"Where do you think you're going?" Iain growled as he followed close behind her.

"Tyra is in danger!" she yelled.

It turned out Yesenda was right, and it was her healing skills and Lachlan Gair's quick thinking that saved Tyra's life.

Claymores

SEVERAL HOURS LATER, once the danger had passed, and things had settled within the glen and the Keep, another unwelcome visitor arrived.

"Iain!" Liosa said as she came barging into the healer's cottage. I heard that the Keep was attacked. Are you well? I was so worried about you." She began fussing over him, and Iain looked slightly embarrassed.

"I am fine," he grunted, but seeing the death stares directed his way from the women, he tried to usher her out of the cottage. "Liosa, I'll meet you outside."

While they were talking, Yesenda did not say a word. She was still reeling from Liosa's presence. Because Liosa was wearing the garment Yesenda had seen draped over the chair in the blackhouse. It was confirmation that Liosa was having an affair with a man who wasn't Iain. She was not to be trusted. Yesenda warred with several emotions, jealousy, concern and suspicion.

When Iain moved to follow Liosa out the door, Yesenda smirked. On his way out Iain asked what she was smirking at and Yesenda said, "Be careful where you sheath your claymore, Warrior." She delivered it with a grin, but she was deadly serious about her statement.

Iain stilled for a moment in shock at her words, then he threw his head back and roared with laughter. Yesenda savored it shoring up precious moments to last a lifetime.

She had just turned to get back to her task when Iain appeared before her again.

He lowered his voice so the others would not hear him.

Iain bent and whispered in her ear, "There is much you have kept from me, but ken this, love, I will have all your secrets."

Then he was gone. Yesenda exhaled the breath she was holding.

LATER THAT NIGHT, YESENDA tossed and turned in her bed. The attack from the *Brotherhood* still reeling in her head. Too many missing pieces. She felt the need to remain vigilant, but she was bone weary. The *Brotherhood* wanted her dead and that meant everyone around her was in danger.

She could not go to Edmund now in the event someone was watching her and she could not remain and attract danger. She needed to find out who wanted her dead and eliminate the threat.

Yesenda noticed Iain had not returned after escorting Liosa to the village. That disturbed her the most. Were they coupling? Were they together again? Is this what life would be like, always wondering where Iain was every time Liosa entered their lives again? She really needed to pull herself together. Lives were at stake, and she was thinking only of her own feelings.

Chapter 12

Ticklish

Iain returned to the glen late. He made sure Liosa stayed in the village and away from his kin. He was becoming increasingly annoyed by her constant presence. She tried several times to talk him into taking her back, but his only concern was getting back to Yesenda. He had so many questions to ask, like who taught her to fight like that? Who was Miriam Ferguson? Now that the crisis was over, they needed to have a serious talk about their future.

One thing was for sure, she was like no woman he had ever known and he knew, down to his soul, that she was the type of woman he wanted by his side. She was complex in her simplicity and utterly captivating. Iain wanted her in all the ways he could have her, and that wanting only increased the more he came to know her.

Which is why ten minutes later, he was climbing through the window of her cottage. It was dark, and he saw her in the moonlight, fast asleep. He just gazed at her on the bed and a fierce need to claim her stole over him.

Before he could second guess his actions, he removed his leine and joined her on the bed. She must have been exhausted because she slept through it. He shifted her into a comfortable position and wrapped his body around hers. Then he fell into a peaceful sleep.

He planned to speak to her in the morning, but unfortunately, that plan was derailed.

YESENDA WOKE FEELING refreshed. She hadn't realized how exhausted she was with worry. Yet she somehow fell into a deep sleep. It was dawn when she opened her eyes and she smiled when she smelled that masculine, woodsy scent. It reminded her of Iain. She rubbed her eyes, adjusting to the faint light of dawn, and was just about to turn onto her back when she felt an arm draped across her waist. Yesenda stilled and her first thought was of the *Brotherhood*. In a swift move, she grabbed the arm, pulled hard and twisted her hip, throwing whoever was in bed over the side.

"What the hell?" Iain roared as he landed on the floor with a loud thud.

"Iain?" Yesenda cried out as she peered over the bed. He was flat on his back, staring up at the rafters and blinking in shock.

"Iain!" she shouted and jumped off the bed, trying to help him up. "I am sorry. I thought it was someone else."

He growled as he sat up. "Who else were you expecting to share your bed?"

"No one. I just meant I thought it was an enemy."

"Well, clearly tis not! You nearly broke my skull." He grabbed her hand as she pulled him up to standing.

"Is this what I'm going to expect every time I share your bed?" He sat down on the bed, still grumbling.

"Iain, why were you in my bed? I could've killed you."

"Aye, you almost did, you blood thirsty wench!" He scowled at her.

"I'm sorry. I was not expecting to find you in my bed. Why are you here?"

"Can't a man sneak into his woman's bed without having his neck broken?" he snapped.

Yesenda could not help it. Something about the way Iain was grumbling gave her the giggles. He was a sight. His short hair was sticking up in different directions. His trews were riding low, and he was rubbing the back of his neck. She bit her lip and tried to not laugh, but her belly and shoulders started shaking with mirth.

"Are you laughing because you nearly killed me in my sleep?" He frowned.

She shook her head and tried to keep a straight face.

"Aye, you are laughing at me," Iain said suddenly seeing the humor of what just transpired.

"No, I am not laughing at you, Iain," Yesenda said, then snorted and covered her mouth.

"You think it's funny, do you, lass? I'll show you funny," Iain said. Before Yesenda could do anything, Iain pulled her onto the bed and rolled her onto her back. He was lying on top, caging her in. Then he tickled her.

"Iain!" she shrieked and burst into a fit of giggles. She was trying to stop his hands but losing the battle.

"Ah, my woman has a weakness. She is ticklish," he said as he tickled her some more.

Yesenda screamed with laughter, and Iain could not help himself. He started chuckling, enjoying her torment.

"Stop, Iain, I cannot breathe," she rasped, then kept giggling.

"Do you yield?" he asked.

"Aye, I yield. I yield!"

He stopped tickling her, and instead, he caressed her cheek with the back of his hand.

"Then I require a boon," he whispered.

"What boon?"

They were both still now.

"A kiss from a bonnie lass."

"Oh, well, if you let me up, I'll go find one for you," Yesenda joked.

But Iain was not laughing. He was gazing at her with penetrating dark eyes filled with hunger. "I dinnae want just any lass. Only you," he said as he brushed his lips softly against hers.

Yesenda suddenly felt as if she could not breathe. She was aware of Iain's body above hers. She could feel his hard length through his trews as it rested against her thigh.

She moaned and lifted her face, closing the distance between them, and she captured his mouth with hers.

Iain growled and rolled them until she was on top. He held her tight and deepened the kiss. They were both panting, and their hands were caressing each other's bodies.

"Iain?" she whimpered.

"Aye, love?"

"I need more," she said as she ground her hips against him.

He groaned and threw his head back, savoring the sensation caused by the friction against his length.

He was going to give her more when he heard the pounding on the door.

"Yesenda? Tis Kieran."

"Go away!" Iain shouted just as Yesenda slammed her palm across his mouth to keep him quiet.

"Iain? I suggest you get out of there because Bram is on his way, and he wants a word with Yesenda."

Yesenda jumped out of the bed, practically pushing Iain out of the way. She grabbed some clothes and ran out the door with only her chemise on.

"Where are you going?" Iain yelled.

"I need a cold bath in the river. I cannot meet Bram like this," she shouted back.

Iain noticed her face was flushed, and she looked as if she had just been ravished.

He looked down and noticed he was still semi-aroused.

"Wait!" Iain picked up his leine. "I also need a dip in the river."

Kieran just shook his head as Iain ran after Yesenda. "I swear the people in this clan are bloody daft," he muttered to himself.

Ten minutes later Iain and Yesenda both emerged with wet hair donning a change of clothes and they had lost the 'hazed over with lust' expression.

BRAM QUESTIONED YESENDA thoroughly about the *Brotherhood* and why they thought of attacking Henderson Keep. She gave them mostly half-truths and assured him she would move on as soon as she could so as not to endanger anyone else. Bram and Iain disagreed with her. They believed the crisis had passed, and they were safer if they all stuck together. Yesenda let it go. She would just have to remain vigilant.

As for the subject of Miriam Ferguson, Yesenda outright lied that she knew nothing of the woman, and it was most likely mistaken identity. She felt guilty about lying to them, but she had no choice. When grilled about her fighting abilities, she told more half-truths, explaining that the abbey taught the nuns self-defense in the event of an attack. Bram and Iain found that a plausible explanation and, to Yesenda's relief, they dropped the matter.

Chasing Waterfalls

YESENDA SLIPPED OUT of the Keep early in the morning, hoping to find a secluded spot to bathe.

Sorcha told her of a waterfall close to the Keep. When she reached it on foot, she was so excited. She discarded her clothes and jumped straight in. Ten minutes later, she had rinsed off the soap and was frolicking in the water when she heard someone approaching. She had no time to hide, so she ducked underwater and swam towards a boulder. She surfaced and treaded water, waiting.

Yesenda heard a splash and the telltale sounds of someone bathing. She wanted to shout out that she was there, but not knowing whether they were friend or foe, she refrained. Yesenda quietly swam around, trying to get a glimpse, and stilled when she saw the glorious sight of Iain Henderson completely naked. He was standing waist deep in water, his body lathered with soap, and he had his eyes closed, rinsing his hair under the smaller waterfall.

Yesenda felt her face heat. She should have alerted him to her presence, but she could not look away. The water cascaded down his muscular arms to his solid chest and down his chiseled stomach. Yesenda had visions of caressing every inch of his body. She felt her nipples harden and a tingling sensation strike at her core. Her cheeks flushed.

Afraid of getting discovered ogling his body, she quietly retreated to her side of the pool, making as little noise as possible. When she reached the water's edge, she slowly hefted herself up and stood on a rock ledge. She was reaching for a drying cloth when she heard a voice say, "What the devil?"

Yesenda turned, then realized to her horror it was Iain, standing a few feet away, completely naked. He gazed at her body. Yesenda gasped and quickly covered her breasts with one arm and her quim with one hand, then she backed away. Not thinking about the rocks and the steep drop behind her.

"Stop!" Iain shouted and rapidly closed the distance between them. Yesenda teetered backward on the verge of falling down the incline just as Iain grabbed her and pulled her towards him. They both toppled into the water, with Iain wrapped around her.

When they surfaced, Iain had his arms about her in a protective hold. He held her close and said, "Are you all right?"

"Aye, I'm sorry. I was bathing and did not realize anyone else was coming..."

"Tis all right, love. I thought I heard a noise."

"I'm sorry, tis my fault I should have called out but I—"

"No, truly it was my fault, I um—"

They both stopped talking when they realized they were naked and in a rock pool. Their faces were inches apart, their bodies touching under the surface.

Iain gritted his teeth and willed himself not to become aroused, but the scent of her permeated his senses. His arms remained around her and couldn't help but noticed how perfectly she fit against him.

He could feel her taut nipples rubbing against his chest, and he groaned.

Yesenda had her arms around Iain, and she gloried in the feel of him. Then she felt his hands moving and caressing her back.

Iain could not help himself. Yesenda haunted his dreams at night and now she was there in the flesh. The sound of her ragged breaths told him she was not unaffected by either.

He leaned closer and dipped his mouth towards her neck so he could inhale her scent. Yesenda raised her languid eyelids and stared directly into his. Iain saw something there. A burning need that reflected his own. A wanting he felt compelled to satisfy.

"Iain," she whispered. "You should probably let me go now."

"Aye, I should. But I dinnae want to."

She blushed, then tried to lower her eyes, but he clasped her chin and raised her head to look at him.

"You're beautiful Yesenda. The bonniest woman I've ever laid my eyes upon."

"You're beautiful too, Iain." Yesenda brushed the back of her palm across his jaw.

He chuckled then said, "Och lass dinnae you mean I am braw and handsome?"

"No, I meant what I said. You are everything a man should be."

Iain stilled as those words pierced through the fog and the armor. No woman had ever looked at him like he was everything.

"Damn it to hell," he whispered. Iain kissed her then, and Yesenda welcomed it by opening her mouth as their tongues intertwined.

Iain tightened his hold, deepening the kiss, and Yesenda wrapped her arms around him. She could feel his hardened length prodding her belly, and while it surprised her, she was not afraid. Yesenda was lost in the moment's bliss. She moved her hand lower to caress his length when instinct alerted her to danger.

Yesenda saw movement behind Iain as a man emerged from the clearing.

She broke the kiss and pushed Iain out of the way just as a sharp dagger came flying. She dodged it, then hauled herself up onto the rock and hurled her body at their attacker. Her body weight forced the assailant backward, and he landed on the ground with a thud.

"Yesenda!" Iain shouted, and she could hear him clambering out behind her. Get out of the way and put clothes on."

She ignored Iain and punched the assailant in the face. Before Yesenda could do anything else, Iain physically lifted her and shoved her to the side.

She watched in awe as a very muscular Iain unleashed his fists on the man. He picked him up by the scruff of his neck and broke his jaw, then threw him onto the ground. The man was writhing in pain after his head hit a rock.

Yesenda ran for her tunic and donned it, then she grabbed Iain's plaid and dagger. Iain was now standing over the unconscious culprit. She handed him his garments, which he quickly donned, and she tried hard not to look below the belt.

Yesenda saw a different side to Iain. One of a Highland Warrior. He was furious; the anger etched in his facial expressions.

Then he turned to her and... exploded. "What the bloody hell did you think you were doing?" he shouted.

"Me? I was trying to save you—"

"You pushed me out of the way and threw your naked body at him."

"Aye, I did?"

"Dinnae ever do something like that again. You could have been killed!"

"Iain," she whispered, trying to placate him.

"And naked! You attacked him buck naked."

"Well, twas necessary—"

"Twas unnecessary. Have you no sense, woman?"

"I was in no danger," she snapped, tired of Iain's attitude.

"Never throw yourself at an attacker. Do you understand? Tis my job to protect you."

"But I was perfectly fine to—"

"No, you were not! Good lord, woman, you were naked."

"So, what?"

"I am the only man who gets to see you naked, do you hear me?" he growled.

"That's why you're angry?"

Iain huffed and ignored her, and turned his attention to the assailant. The man was losing too much blood and began spluttering.

"Who sent you?" Iain asked.

"*Manus Dei,*" he said before he died.

"What does that mean?" Iain asked.

"Hand of God," Yesenda replied as she made the sign of the cross.

Iain's entire body stiffened, and he could barely see through the panic and haze. He knew it had to do with Yesenda. His protective instinct towards her increased one hundred-fold.

Yesenda rushed to dress and Iain followed suit. He was quiet and contemplative. When he was ready, he clasped her hand and pulled her behind him. Yesenda followed, sensing Iain's need for quiet.

"Where is your horse?" he asked.

"I walked."

He stopped. "You walked! By yourself, all the way out here?" he hissed.

"Aye."

Iain shook his head, took a deep breath, then placed his hands around her waist and hoisted her onto his horse. Then he jumped up behind her, wrapped his plaid around her and pulled her tight to his chest.

"From now on, you go nowhere without me. Do you hear me?" Iain said.

Yesenda just sighed heavily.

Iain repeated louder, "Do you hear me, Yesenda?"

"Aye. I'm sure even the pope in Rome heard you!" she snapped.

"Dinnae try my patience," he snapped back.

She rolled her eyes, wondering how a blissful moment of intimacy could turn into this.

The Blackhouse

THE PILGRIM REMAINED calm, but he was seething inside. "Why are you here, Liosa?"

"Your men have failed again. She lives and there are more guardsmen teeming about."

"Then tell me what you know," the pilgrim said.

"I ken where she will be during the days. She follows a loose routine. I have been watching her. If you mean to capture her, it will have to be at one of those moments where she is most vulnerable."

"And when is she most vulnerable?" he asked.

"When she is around the bairns. She would die to protect them."

Chapter 13

Wreck and Ruin

As things settled again, Yesenda awaited further instructions from the abbey, but nothing came. She even managed a sneak away to the blackhouse and the Gibson farm, but both were empty. So, she decided she would remain one more week to make sure she was not followed. Given that she was to leave soon, she tried once more to keep her distance from Iain, but each morning when she awoke; she found him asleep in her bed and curled around her. Although he never pushed for anything more. The connection between them was growing stronger, but she could not give herself to a man, knowing that she would have to leave him forever.

In hindsight, Yesenda wished she had savored those quiet moments wrapped in his arms because things were about to take a drastic turn in their relationship.

News

YESENDA WAS WAITING for Iain at the Keep when Kieran appeared.

"Yesenda, Iain has clan matters today. I'll walk you home."

Kieran ushered her forward, and they set off for the glen.

"Thank you, Kieran. I haven't seen you in a while."

"Aye, I've been a little busy." He frowned.

"Is this related to a certain widow in the village?" Yesenda raised her eyebrow and kept winking at him.

"Och, is nothing a secret to this clan?" Kieran grumbled.

Yesenda laughed. She heard the clanswomen gossiping about Kieran that morning. Apparently, his latest love interest was slightly weird.

Yesenda asked, "Is it true then? The lass really made you burn your plaid to remove the evil eye curse?"

"Aye, she did. She said she had to transfer all the evil from *an droch-shùil,* into me plaid and not just a thread of yarn."

"Was there affliction? Did someone really put the evil eye on you both?" Yesenda asked.

"Of course not! The lass may be bonnie, but she is daft like all the women I seem to attract."

Yesenda sobered and asked, "So, what happened afterwards?"

"Well, she set my plaid alight so all the evil would vanish, and it caught fire to my trews, which were hanging by the window. So I come home last night and my cottage is on fire."

Yesenda tried hard to stifle her laugh. "So that's why you've all been busy rebuilding."

"Aye. What I would not give to have a bonnie sweet woman who doesna frighten the life out of me half the time."

"You wish to wed. Kieran?"

"Aye, I do."

"I thought you were happy to be single and have your way with as many women as you please."

He snorted. "It used to be enough. But sometimes I wish I had a lass to come home to and bairns underfoot. But every time I find one, she either nearly gets me killed or burns my house down."

"Mayhap I could find a bonnie MacDonald lass for you to wed. There are plenty of beauties in my clan and—"

"No!" Kieran said.

"What do you mean 'no'? You've never met any of them."

"I've met you and that's plenty enough."

"Kieran, I am shocked. I'll have you ken MacDonald lassies are the finest women you'll ever meet!"

Kieran just snorted.

Yesenda felt the insult. "What's your last name again?" she asked.

"MacKenzie."

"Oh well, you're right. A MacKenzie will not do for my clanswomen."

Kieran looked affronted. "What is wrong with MacKenzies?"

"Nothing but *bawbags,* the lot of them. I think tis best you dinnae marry into my clan. The women would spurn your advances," she snapped.

Kieran just chuckled. It was the first time he had seen Yesenda get her back up and he found it hilarious.

They had just reached the wooden pathway to the longhouse when Yesenda sensed someone close by. She whipped her head around just in time to see a hooded figure land a couple of feet away.

Kieran immediately put his body in front of hers and drew his sword.

"Calm down, warrior, I mean you no harm," a woman said. She removed her hood to reveal herself.

"Naomi!" Yesenda leapt with joy and ran to embrace her.

"Why are you jumping out of trees?" Kieran growled.

Naomi ignored him. "Yesenda, I've got an urgent message from the abbey."

Kieran watched the exchange, part enamored, and part annoyed to be dismissed so easily.

Yesenda asked, "What has happened?"

Naomi glanced at Kieran and then at Yesenda, signaling that she could say nothing until Kieran moved away.

Kieran sheathed his sword and folded his arms. "Whatever you have to say can be said right here in front of me."

Naomi flashed him an angry look, and Kieran just raised his eyebrow mockingly.

"Kieran, this is my friend from the abbey. She obviously needs to relay an important message. Might we have some privacy?"

"No!" he said. "I am to guard you until Iain returns and I'll not let you out of my sight."

Yesenda had forgotten how stubborn Kieran could be.

Naomi asked Kieran, "So, you are her guard, are you?"

"Aye, I am."

"Naomi moved so fast it took Kieran by surprise. She pulled a staff from her cloak, spun it, took two steps and whacked his arm. Then she poked the stick end at his stomach. "Pfft, some guard you are," she snorted.

"Naomi," Yesenda warned. "Dinnae be rude."

"Och, lass. Do you mean to impress me with your... *stick*?" Kieran scoffed and in an even faster move, he grabbed the end and pulled it so forcefully, Naomi made a startled cry as she came with it. With a few quick moves, Kieran had her back against his chest and his arms clamped hard against her front, keeping her in place with her own staff. Try as she might, Naomi could not free herself.

Kieran smugly whispered in her ear, "Your turn."

Naomi felt a shiver go through her, but anger quickly replaced it. Before Kieran could say another word, she lifted her foot and slammed her heel down on his shoe.

"Damn it to hell!" he cursed, and let her go as he limped backward.

Naomi smirked and mimicked, "Your turn."

"Naomi! That is enough. Kieran, please give me some privacy. She is no threat."

"Hmph, maybe not to you," he grumbled, but stepped a few feet away. Then he glared at Naomi, who poked her tongue out at him.

"Naomi, what has happened?"

"A message from Brother Mateo."

"Oh, praise be. Finally, some word. Is he well?"

"Aye, he is well, but he asks that you remain in Scotland with your charge," Naomi whispered the last part.

"And what of Abbess Murdina? Did she send you?"

"Um ah well no, not really."

"Naomi?" Yesenda warned.

"All right. Mother Abbess has gone to Normandy. She left two weeks ago. Sister Bissett did not trust anyone else to deliver the message, so she asked me to do it."

Yesenda nodded, then asked. "How are things at the abbey?"

"Not good. Something strange is happening. Even Sister Bissett seems on edge, and she is usually always calm."

"I wonder why that is."

"There's one more thing. After you left, a warrior came searching for Miriam Ferguson."

"What did he want?"

"He said she had something that belonged to his liege. Twas not material possession but something more. We sent him on his way, but then..."

"Then what?"

"After Abbess Murdina left, a French woman sought shelter at the abbey. She stayed a few days."

"What was her name?"

"She said her name was Charlotte, but I didna believe it. I hid in the gardens one day when she was talking to her companion and I overheard the other woman call her 'Matilda,' then apologize for the slip. Something about her has me worried."

Yesenda said, "I must leave here soon, and you must return to the abbey under escort. Tis not safe for you to travel alone."

Kieran eventually moved closer, and he asked, "Naomi, how did you get here?"

"The usual way by land and a road."

"By yourself?"

"*Si.*"

"You travelled alone? From the abbey?"

"*Si,*" Naomi said.

"Are you daft? Tis dangerous on the roads for a lone woman." He frowned.

Naomi just shrugged and said, "Not when I am dressed like a man."

Kieran clenched his jaw and raked her body from head to toe, then said, "Believe me, I have a good eye, and it would not take long before someone saw past your disguise to the feminine curves beneath."

"You're only saying that because you know I am a woman now. But if I walked past you in a village with my hood up, you would not even recognize me."

"Trust me, lass, I ken a woman when I see one, and it has nothing to do with your hood."

Naomi blushed.

Then Kieran said, "I will escort you back to the abbey myself."

Yesenda raised her eyebrow at that suggestion.

Naomi said, "You will do no such thing. You'll only slow me down, you behemoth."

"We'll see about that," Kieran said.

THAT AFTERNOON, YESENDA made plans to leave Henderson land. She needed to get to Edmund because it seemed their enemies were closing in. She did not know how she was going to break the news to Iain, but she had to trust her instincts. As a member of the *Order*, her vow came first above all things. Even the longings of her own heart.

Naomi spent the rest of the day with Yesenda, which gave them time to plan a means for Yesenda to slip away quietly.

Yesenda was packing her belongings at the longhouse when the Henderson children dropped by to visit. They asked her to play a game of *'Hoodman's Blind'* with them in the field behind the cottages. Yesenda was about to refuse, then she realized she would probably never see Mysie, Domhnall, or Michael again once she left. They sat with her every night when she and Iain partook of the evening meal at the Keep. She cared for them.

"All right," she said. "Just one game, then we best get ready for supper."

Their faces lit up as Mysie ran to find a piece of cloth for the game.

Thirty minutes and three games later, Michael wore the blindfold, and they were all running around him laughing as he tried to tag the next 'It'.

Some passersby from the village also stopped to join in the fun.

Iain was returning to the longhouse on horseback when he saw the game in play. He could not help but grin at the merriment of the participants, especially Yesenda. Her cheeks were flushed, and her facial expression joyful. The children were running and screaming, and she looked perfectly content amidst the frivolity. Iain thought she was the most beautiful woman on earth.

He was watching her closely when her smile suddenly vanished, and her eyes darted toward the trees. Her entire body went rigid, and so did Iain's. Then he saw what caught Yesenda's attention. Arrows let loose and aimed at the children. His heart lodged in his throat when he saw Yesenda running straight into the line of fire, and he roared.

Chapter 14

Lies by Omission

Iain spurred his horse into motion when he saw arrows hurtling through the air towards the children. He roared, "Get down!"

The onlookers turned their attention to Iain, so they missed something far more incredible. But Iain did not miss a beat because he kept his eyes focused on Yesenda.

Mysie, Michal and Domhnall were within reach of each other and directly in the line of fire.

Yesenda ran at Mysie, grabbed the back of her dress, and pulled her away from one arrow. She then sprinted towards a blindfolded Michael and shoved him onto the ground. Then, in a move that seemed almost unworldly, she pivoted, lunged forward and caught the arrow shaft with her hand, preventing it from hitting Domhnall. The motion propelled her forward, and she hit the ground, then rolled into a crouch position.

Yesenda discarded the arrow, then Iain watched her pull something from her leg stare at the tree line, then she took off in a sprint straight for the trees.

"No!" he roared. "Stay where you are!" But she ignored him.

Iain veered his horse in her direction.

He yelled to the others to see to the children, then he took off after Yesenda. Iain was just bringing up the rear when he watched her hurl a dagger into the air. He heard a loud oomph sound then rustling leaves before a body fell out of the tree. It landed with a thud a few feet away. A dagger lodged between the man's eyes.

"Bloody hell, woman!"

He had seen no one achieve that before. Her reflexes were quicker than any mans.

As Iain pieced things together, he knew right down to his soul, Yesenda had lied to them all.

Yesenda emerged soon after from the tree line, and Iain did not hesitate. He rode towards her, his expression one of anger, and in one swoop he had her on his horse. Then he clicked his heels, and they rode back to the cottages.

"Iain! Put me down."

"Be quiet!" he growled and tightened his grip.

When they reached his men, he issued orders to retrieve the body and secure the area.

By the time he reached the cottages, his fear for Yesenda's was replaced with something he had not felt in a long time. *Rage.*

It startled Yesenda when Iain jumped down from his horse and plucked her off the saddle. They saw to the children to make sure they were all right and then Iain announced, "Yesenda and I need to talk, then we will all return to the Keep."

The children nodded while they sat in the safety of the longhouse.

Iain grabbed Yesenda's arm and dragged her towards his cottage.

"Iain? What is the matter with you?"

He could not speak; he was seething now. Iain clenched his jaw so hard he thought it would break.

"Iain? Unhand me."

"Shut your mouth before I strip you in-front of everyone and tan your hide raw."

She shut her mouth. He nudged her through the cottage door and slammed it shut, then said, "Start talking because I am hanging by a very thin thread. Who are you?"

"I dinnae ken what you mean, Iain."

"Wrong! Try again," he bellowed. "Who are you? Who was that dead man? And why do men keep trying to kill you?"

"Iain, you need to calm down. Tis not good for your health—"

He stepped closer, towering above her, and said, "So help me, love. Dinnae lie, or I swear you will not walk for a week once I take you over my knee. How does a woman raised in an abbey learn to catch bloody arrows and hurl knives into trees!" he roared.

"Iain, keep your voice down. People will think you are upset."

"I am bloody upset!" he yelled. Then started pacing.

"Iain, there is a lot about me you cannot ken. I have made vows and I cannot break them because other people depend on me to keep them safe. I dinnae mean to upset you, but tis just the way it is."

"Someone nearly killed you and the bairns. No secret is worth your life, Yesenda. God's blood, he could have killed you today."

"Aye, I'll need to leave. I am a danger to be around."

"Why?" he shouted. "Tell me why?" Iain was seriously losing his mind.

"I cannot tell anyone. I didna mean for you to see that."

"Well, I cannot unsee it now, can I?"

"Iain, please understand. I never meant to lie to anyone. I just dinnae give all the information. Anyone who is near me is in danger. It is better if I leave."

"But I can help you if you just tell me."

"No, you cannot. Tis not your burden to bear."

Iain took a deep breath and glared at her. Then he sighed and sat down on the chair.

"Iain?"

When he next spoke, Yesenda knew she could not remain with this man. She would only cause him more pain, and he deserved better than that.

"I spent years pining for a woman who could not be honest with me. But fool that I am, I accepted it because having her anyway I could have her was better than nothing."

"Iain, I dinnae need to hear this."

He continued. "I thought that would be my life. I thought somehow that was the best I could have. A woman who constantly lied to me and made me feel worthless. And then..." He took a deep breath. "And then I met you and finally, after years in purgatory, I had a glimpse of heaven."

"Iain," Yesenda whispered as her expression softened.

"But it's not heaven at all, tis just a different kind of hell because I cannot trust her either. You have been lying to me from the first moment we met. And yet, I refuse to let you face whatever this danger is, alone."

He stood and started pacing and brushing his fingers through his hair. "Good lord, I must be all kinds of a fool."

"Iain, you need to let me go," Yesenda said. She clasped his hand and pulled him to face her. "You need to let me go. You deserve better and I am not it."

He just shook his head. His facial expression held pain when he said, "No."

Iain kept staring at Yesenda, then he took a deep breath and said, "But you're right. I deserve the best. By the gods, I have fucking earned it. If I have to do this, then so be it."

Yesenda closed her eyes and nodded.

She opened them when Iain asked, "These vows you took, are you a nun dedicated for life at the abbey?"

She shook her head and said, "No, tis not like that. I am free to live anywhere."

"So you can marry and have bairns someday?"

"Aye, but why are you asking me this?"

"I need something to look forward to in my future."

"What do you mean?"

"Well, seeing as you dinnae trust me enough to tell me your secrets, I have to prove that I am trustworthy. So, I am coming with you."

Yesenda's mouth dropped open, and she stared at Iain as if he'd lost his mind.

"But first, we're getting married so you cannot hie off somewhere without me."

"What the—"

Iain ignored her and instead grabbed her hand and dragged her out of the cottage. He walked with purposeful strides to get the children.

"Iain! What are you doing?"

"I'm hungry, and I ken the bairns are, too. They've had a trying day."

"But I need to—"

"Yesenda, the bairns are hungry and upset. Please stop being selfish and put your problems aside for now."

"My proble—"

"Mysie, Domhnall, Michael, come help your aunt Yesenda. She could do with some hugs."

The children ran to Yesenda and crowded around her. She hugged them and gave Iain a death glare when the children were not looking. He just ignored her.

Council Room, Henderson Keep

IAIN EXPLAINED EVERYTHING to Bram, who issued orders for his War Band to increase guards and patrols. Iain explained about what happened with Yesenda and the children."

"Bram, I've seen no one move as fast as she did today. She is highly skilled in combat, whether it be hand to hand or with weapons. There is no way I could have saved three bairns like she did today."

"How did she do it?"

"She pulled Mysie out of the path of one arrow. Shoved Michael onto the ground, and then she caught the shaft of another arrow with her bare hand before it hit Domhnall."

"Damn, that is mighty impressive. Mayhap she should be the one training our warriors."

"Aye, I agree." Iain was quiet for a while.

"So what is troubling you, Iain?" Bram asked.

"Yesenda put her body in the line of fire to protect the bairns with no thought to her own safety. It filled my heart with warmth that she would protect our kin, but it also fills me with dread. Someday she may not be fast enough to stop the arrows."

"But there's more?"

"She lied to all of us. To me. She's been lying the whole time pretending to be this gently reared fragile lass, when she is anything but. Tis the fact that she lies about who she is that doesna sit well with me."

"But was she pretending to be a fragile woman? Or is that what we assumed?"

Iain said, "A lie is still a lie if you hold back important facts."

"Iain, what is this really about?" It amazed Iain that Bram could read him so well.

"You asked me once what I'd do if Yesenda left."

"Aye, you said you'd follow her to the end of the earth and drag her back. Is that still true?"

"It is, but I am torn with the need to protect her and not wanting to leg shackle myself to another Liosa."

"Yesenda is not Liosa. You do her no favors by comparing the two."

"But *she lied to me* about who she is. Even now I dinnae have the full picture."

Bram said, "And what were the reasons? She made a vow to someone, and she means to uphold it."

"She should trust me with it."

"And then what? You would make her change course, something she cannot do."

Iain was silent a moment.

Then Bram said, "All it shows is that Yesenda is loyal and when her oath is pledged, she keeps it. We dinnae ken the full story, but she does, and by the sounds of it, she is well trained to deal with the consequences."

"I love her, Bram."

"I ken it, Iain."

"I'm scared that the woman I love is a lie."

"Cousin, for years you've had the wrong woman in your bed. She convinced you that you deserved no better. I am telling you; you deserve better. And right now, that 'better' is getting ready to hie off without you. So, you can sit here drowning in self-pity or you can embrace a future with a woman who would die to protect you and your kin."

"Aye, you're right. Send the missive. Let Ruadh ken what is happening."

"Are you sure, Iain?" Bram asked.

"I'm sure."

"Then consider it done. But if you give me a few days, I can come with you."

"No, our clan needs its laird, and you've got a wife and bairn to think about now. But I thank you for being prepared to help."

"At least wait a couple of days," Bram said.

"I cannot do that. I ken Yesenda is going to leave in the morn without me."

"Then I wish you Godspeed Iain. Be safe."

Naomi's Room, Henderson Keep

"YESENDA, ARE YOU SURE this is going to work?"

"Aye, you just play your part, Naomi, and no one will be the wiser."

"I thought we were going to wait until the morning."

"I've run out of time."

"All right, I'm coming with you."

"No, I need you to get back to the abbey. Wait there for Abbess Murdina and please allow Kieran to escort you home."

"Yesenda, if I have to put up with that *uomo scontroso* all the way to the abbey, he is going to end up with a staff up his arse."

Yesenda chuckled. "Naomi! That is very uncharitable of you. I ken he can be grumpy, but he is a fine warrior. You're safer with him by your side."

"Fine."

THE NEXT MORNING AT the Keep, Iain strode into the Great Hall, waiting to see the look on Yesenda's face, when she realized her plan had failed.

"Morning Iain. What a pleasant surprise. You rarely come to the Keep to break your fast. Are you meeting someone?" Tyra asked. She was sitting, eating her meal with Lachlan.

"Aye, I am waiting for Yesenda to escort her back to the glen."

"Yesenda?" Lachlan asked, looking confused.

"Aye."

"But she's no longer here," Tyra said.

"What do you mean?" Iain asked, feeling a sliver of concern.

Lachlan said, "She left at dusk yestereve. A missive arrived from Ruadh, and two guardsmen, Connor and Diarmid escorted her."

"What!" Iain growled.

The two men in question entered the hall.

Iain said, "Where is Yesenda? Why are you not escorting her?"

"We met a MacDonald retainer along the way, and he said he would take it from there, so we returned."

Iain gritted his teeth and said, "She just pulled the wool over all your eyes."

Connor asked, "How?"

"I bet the retainer is her friend from the abbey."

"That cannot be. I just saw Naomi above stairs," Tyra said.

Iain just shook his head, part prideful that she outplayed him, and part angry at the worry she was causing him now. Iain stormed out of the hall. When he got to the cottage, he packed and gathered provisions, then he saddled his horse and rode out to find the troublesome wench.

A Day Later

THANKS TO HIS FAST pace and excellent tracking skills, Iain had caught up with Yesenda the following day. When he rode over the rise, Yesenda was fighting three men. *Bloody typical,* he thought. He urged his horse into a fast gallop, unsheathed his claymore and shouted a battle cry as he rode towards her.

Yesenda heard Iain riding to her rescue before she saw him. She remained focused on her current attackers as her bronzed head mace clashed against their swords. She tried to reason with them, but they kept repeating that their orders were to kill.

Iain leapt from his horse and was at her side in a heartbeat. He threw himself in the melee as his claymore clashed against steel.

"Gaah! Not again. I cannot leave you alone for a day without you finding trouble. I am sick of this shit," he muttered.

"I warned you, several times, you will not listen. Tis your own damned fault." Yesenda scowled, but deep inside she felt relief. *He did not abandon her.*

They blocked and parried as the three men came at them from different sides.

Yesenda nudged Iain behind her and she realized something important. She had faith that Iain would protect her back as surely as she protected him. They fought as one. With silent communication between them. To fight side by side like that took something more than skill. It required complete trust.

And out there on a dusty road fighting for her life, Yesenda had an epiphany. *I trust Iain.*

By the end of the skirmish, the attackers lay dead.

"This is beyond the pale," Yesenda said as she bent over the dead men, closing their sightless eyes, and offering a silent prayer. "Tis such a waste of life."

Iain nodded but remained silent as he dragged the bodies off the road. When he was atop his horse, he waited for Yesenda to lead the way. He would not demand or ask; he would just follow her lead. Yesenda paused for a moment and then she turned her steed toward *Kentallen.*

Chapter 15

Trust

Several hours later they came by a *bothy* where they would stay the night. They secured the area, built a fire, and settled the horses for the night. Yesenda went down to bathe by the bay while Iain kept vigil. When she emerged, he took his turn.

When Iain walked into the little cottage, he took a sharp intake of breath. Yesenda was wearing a chemise with an *airisaidh* draped over her shoulders. She was preparing food for them both. She set out two trenchers with a variety of food.

He barred the door and realized how small the *bothy* was and her scent, that glorious wildflower scent, assailed him.

Yesenda smiled and said, "I am just preparing a light repast. You must be famished. Come sit down."

He joined her at the table. Yesenda handed him his trencher, then poured him a cup of mulled spice wine she had warmed over the fire.

"Thanks, sweeting," he said.

She blushed, then sat down in the chair beside him. They gave thanks and enjoyed their humble fare.

Iain sipped the mulled wine and savored the taste. "Lass, this wine is delicious. What did you add to it?"

"Just some dried orange, cinnamon, and cloves from the abbey."

"It warms my belly and my heart."

They fell into a comfortable silence, just enjoying each other's company and the quiet.

When the meal was over, Yesenda cleaned and packed away their provisions. Then they sat by the fire and sipped their wine.

"Iain?"

"Aye."

"Are you not curious about where we are going?"

"No."

"Why not?"

"Because I trust you'll tell me when you're ready."

Her expression softened. "You're a good man, Iain Henderson."

Iain smiled and sipped his wine. It struck Yesenda how handsome he was, especially when his eyes warmed and gazed at her.

Iain loved this time with Yesenda. She was not one to talk for the sake of it. It was rare to find a woman who was comfortable with silence. Iain thought about Liosa and how she never stopped talking. She needed to be entertained all the time and some days he found it exhausting.

Yesenda was not sure whether it was the mulled wine spices or the pleasant evening, but she felt full to bursting with joy that Iain was with her, and she blurted it out. "Iain, I am happy you are here."

"So am I, love."

After some time passed Iain said, "Yesenda, put your wine on the table."

"Why?" she asked, confused.

"Just do it."

She did.

Iain gave her a wry grin, then he reached across and plucked her off her chair and placed her on his lap.

"Iain!"

"That's better," he said, ignoring her. He wrapped his arms about her and settled.

"Iain, I have a perfectly good seat over there."

"You were too far away. This is better."

Yesenda just shook her head, but she did not protest. In fact, she rested her head in the crook of his neck. Then they watched the fire together.

"Yesenda?"

"Aye."

"Tis time for bed." Iain gazed at her with hunger in his eyes. He lifted her off the chair and carried her to the bed, then placed her down in front of it.

"Iain, I need to tell you something."

He moved closer; his mouth brushed against hers. "Aye love."

"I dinnae think we should... touch."

"You dinnae want us to touch?" he asked as his hand caressed her cheek.

"No..." she squeaked.

"Why not Yesenda? You dinnae like it?" He leaned in and kissed her neck.

"Aye, I dinnae like it," she said breathlessly.

"Why?" He brushed the back of his hand across her breast.

"Because..." she rasped.

"Because?" he asked as he lowered his head and licked the taut peak through the material.

"Iain!"

"Hmm?" he mumbled as he lowered the front of her chemise, baring her to his hungry gaze.

"Oh, my..."

"You dinnae want me to touch you here?" he asked. He laved one peak with his tongue.

Yesenda threw her head back and moaned.

"Or is it here where you dinnae want me to touch you?" He lavished attention on the other one.

Her legs gave out from under her. One moment she was standing, the next she was in Iain's arms as he lowered her onto the bed and followed her down.

"I have something to tell you, too. I am going to touch you as much as I like because you're mine," he said.

Yesenda clasped his hands to stop him from caressing her skin. "But we are not married, Iain."

He frowned. "And whose bloody fault is that? I told you we needed to marry before we left. By tradition, it could have been done with Bram's approval."

"Aye, but I was raised in an abbey, and I want it done the religious way."

He sat up after staring at her for a long time. "All right then. But when we arrive at our destination, the first priest I find is going to marry us. Do you agree?"

She nodded.

"Say it, love. I want your agreement in words."

"Iain, if you can find a priest where we're going, then I will marry you." Yesenda smirked to herself. She knew there were no priests there. Well, none she could find.

Iain said, "Good. Now you better get into that bed and cover yourself up to your neck, so I dinnae ravish you." He kissed her on the lips, then stood and headed for the door.

"Where are you going?"

"To throw myself into the freezing bay!" he grumbled.

Iain closed the door and marched down to the water. He was so hard he was fit to burst. Having Yesenda around him all day was messing with his senses. He needed to remind himself that she was an innocent, and he needed to proceed with care. His one consolation was that she agreed to be his wife if he could find a priest. Iain smiled to himself. The moment Yesenda said I do; she was not leaving his bed for at least a month!

When Iain returned, he warmed himself by the fire, then joined Yesenda on the bed. Her eyes were drooping, and she kept yawning. He settled himself beside her, and she snuggled into his chest. Iain breathed in her alluring scent and felt peace.

As he was drifting off to sleep, Yesenda said, "We are going to *Kentallen*. There's a lad there. His name is Edmund, and I am duty bound to protect him."

Iain gave her arm a small squeeze and kissed the top of her forehead. He heard Yesenda sigh.

"Get some sleep, love," he said. Iain understood the gravity of the moment and the gift Yesenda gave him. *Her trust.*

The Cottages, Kentallen

IAIN AND YESENDA FINALLY arrived at their destination. Yesenda led them down a narrow pathway lined with trees. Iain saw two cottages in the distance.

"The first cottage is where Edmund lives with his parents. The one further up is where we will stay. It has two rooms and backs onto the bay."

As they neared the house, a young lad came outside and waved. A man and woman were behind him. They too smiled in greeting.

They dismounted, and Yesenda did the introductions.

"Edmund, this is Iain Henderson. He will stay with us."

"Is he your man?" Edmund asked, sizing up Iain.

Iain remained silent, letting Yesenda decide what he was to her. His heart warmed when she said, "Aye. He is."

"Is he going to eat all our food? He's huge."

Iain started chuckling. "I brought my own."

"Good then. I dinnae mind if he stays," Edmund said to Yesenda.

Gideon and Sienna just shook their heads.

"These are Edmund's parents."

Iain shook hands and greeted them.

Sienna took Yesenda to the back cottage so she could unload their things and Gideon showed Iain the stable so he could attend to the horses. Later, they gathered for a meal in the main cottage.

"How have things been?" Yesenda asked.

"Very quiet," Gideon replied. "Have you heard any news?"

"Aye, Brother Mateo says we are all to remain here until further notice."

Edmund said, "I dinnae mind it here. I've made some friends; we go fishing sometimes,"

"They're a local family. Their boys are the same age. They have been good company for the lad," Gideon said.

Yesenda smiled, but she could not help but wonder what friends Edmund would have if he were growing up a duke's son. Edmund did not know his lineage. Abbess Murdina said the less a child knows, the less information they're likely to let slip. But Murdina had the records of his parents, their marriage and his birth should Edmund choose to claim his birthright in the future. In the meantime, Gideon trained Edmund to fight and hunting skills while Sienna tutored him in scholastic lessons.

Sienna was a member of the *Order* and when called upon to fulfil a duty, Gideon joined her as well. Gideon loved Sienna and inadvertently married into the Order. They were all part of Murdina's intricate network of people. Yesenda watched the couple as they interacted with Edmund and wondered if Iain would do the same for her someday.

THE FOLLOWING MORNING, Iain said he was going to familiarize himself with the area. He told Yesenda he was uncomfortable being in a strange town until he got his bearings.

Yesenda was busy organizing the cottage and unpacking their provisions, so she nodded and said she would see him later.

It was now later. Yesenda stepped outside to see what all the noise was about. She froze. Iain had returned with a visitor. The man was enormous. He wore a leine and the plaid of his clan. His hair was windswept, his cheeks were ruddy, and he sported a bushy beard. But Yesenda cared little about that. It was the fact the visitor also wore a large cross on a chain around his neck.

When he saw her, he grinned. Then he said in a booming voice, "Och, cousin, she is bonnie to be sure! The lord has been most kind to bless an ugly *muc* like you with such a treasure."

He walked over to Yesenda and gave her a bear hug. "I'm Tavish Stewart, Iain's first cousin on his ma's side, and I'm a priest, but dinnae hold that against me."

Yesenda stammered, "But... I did not think there was clergy in these parts."

"Aye, they're scarce, and you need to ken who they are. You're vera lucky Iain kens these parts well. When he was a lad, he spent most of his summers here by the bay with his kin."

"Did he now?" Yesenda said as she glared at Iain.

Iain just shrugged.

"There's going to be a wedding?" Sienna asked.

"Aye, Yesenda made an *oath* to marry me once I found the first available priest. Well here he is."

Yesenda met Iain's heated gaze and gulped. *Damn it!* She was outplayed.

Hitched

"HERE I GOT YOU THESE," Iain said. He handed Yesenda a small package.

"What is it?"

"Something for you to wear. I picked it up from the village. These are also for you. They belonged to my ma." He handed her a second package. Then he said, "I'll see you at the tree. Dinnae be late." Then he was gone.

Yesenda opened the first package and gasped. It was an embroidered plain crème kirtle with matching slippers. She opened the second package, and it was the Henderson airisaidh and a tiny wooden box. When she lifted the lid, there was a delicate gold band inside. She touched it and felt an overwhelming surge of emotion.

This was her wedding day, and her parents were not going to be there. Her mother would have prepared something for her if she were alive, but Iain gave her everything she needed for her day. The gravity of what this meant hit her hard, and Yesenda burst into tears.

That's how Sienna found her ten minutes later, quietly bawling her eyes out.

"Come on now, lass. Dinnae cry. Come on now. What has you overset?"

Yesenda sobbed, "He got me a dress and his ma's ring. And... I... I have nothing to offer him."

Sienna sat down beside her and said, "I've only met your Highlander recently, but I can tell you this much. That man looks at you like you're his entire world. You say you have nothing to offer, but tis not true. It's *you*, Yesenda. That's all he wants and all he'll ever need."

She sniffed and nodded. "Aye, I will try to be a good wife. No, the best wife for him."

"Och, I doubt you'll need to try. Come on. You have one hour to bathe and dress. You dinnae want your braw highlander kicking the door down and dragging you before the priest, half-dressed, do you?"

Yesenda shook her head. Then had a thought. "Is that what happened at your wedding?"

Sienna replied, "As God is my witness, that's exactly what happened with Gideon. I was taking too long for his liking and let's just say the priest copped an eyeful before I could pull my dress on properly. These men are a different breed. When they want something, nothing will stop them. So, you best dry your eyes and get ready. Hurry before Father Tavish drinks all our mead."

When Yesenda MacDonald finally exchange marriage vows with Iain Henderson, she thought him the handsomest man on earth. His hair was partially wet from his bath, and he wore his full Henderson regalia. It entailed a crisp white leine, his Henderson plaid buckled around his waist and over his shoulder with his crest badge proudly displayed. He wore untanned leather shoes. His polished claymore sheathed in an intricately designed scabbard at his side. But it was the way he gazed at Yesenda when she walked out to meet him beside the tree that stole her breath away. There was so much love shining in his eyes she realized Iain already owned her heart.

Chapter 16

Wedded Bliss

It was their wedding night, and Iain could barely contain his passion. He waited so long to make her his. But he took steady breaths, telling himself he needed to go slow and be gentle. Yesenda had asked that he wait by the fire so she had time to prepare. He refrained from telling her he could prepare her with his hands and his tongue. But if she wanted time, he would give it.

"Iain, you can come in now," she called out.

He took a deep breath and strode into the room He expected to find a shy bride in his bed. Instead, he stilled when he saw her.

"What the devil?" He grunted with an 'oomph' as a very naked Yesenda ran at him. Iain had just enough time to brace and catch her when she leapt into his arms.

Before he could say anything else, her thighs straddled his waist, her breasts pressed up against his chest, and her arms wound about his shoulders.

"Welcome, husband," she rasped before her mouth came crashing down on his.

Iain was undone.

The next moment was a mix between a frenzied attack and absolute bliss. Because as Yesenda kissed him with wild abandon, her fingers were pulling at his garments and discarding them on the floor.

She said, "You have too much on. Take them off."

Iain did not hesitate. He set her feet on the floor, snatching kisses while his hands made fast work of his attire.

Soon, they were both naked and fully bared to one another. Their breathing was labored. Yesenda gasped when she saw the size of his hard length. Her eyes glazed over, and she licked her lips.

Iain's eyes raked her body as his gaze lingered on breasts and the juncture between her thighs. He longed to taste every inch of her. Iain counted to three, then lunged for her. Within seconds, Yesenda was underneath him on the bed and he was hovering above her. Exploring her body with his hands and his mouth.

Iain licked her nipple as he rubbed her pleasure spot between her legs. Yesenda writhed and moaned in pleasure. Her hands caressed his body in returned and Iain cursed when he felt her soft hand wrap around his length and massage him slowly.

Iain groaned and rested his forehead on hers. "I will not last love; I need to be inside you, then we can play another time. I am a big man, so I need to prepare you."

She gazed at him with passion and nodded. Before Yesenda could protest, Iain's head was between her legs. He splayed her thighs apart with his powerful hands, pressing them down against the bed. Then his tongue was on her hooded pearl.

Yesenda felt a visceral sensation shoot from her center to her entire body and she moaned.

Iain continued to pleasure her until she was wet and wanting. Satisfied that she could take him, he crawled back up her body. "I'm going to take you now, love. It may hurt, but I'll be gentle."

Yesenda nodded and spread her legs wider to accommodate his hips. She felt his hard length nudging against her entrance and his ragged breathing. Her body felt like it was on fire.

Iain said, "Guide me, love." She reached down and placed him at her center. Then Iain slowly slid inside her tight, wet sheath. He gritted his teeth to stop from spilling so soon she felt that good. When he felt the barrier, he laved her nipple with his tongue. Yesenda shuddered and moaned and that's when he thrust his way through until he was seated at the hilt.

Her nails dug into his back as she tensed.

Iain gave her a moment to get used to the invasion, then asked, "Are you hale?"

She nodded with a panted breath. Only then did he begin his slow dance of claiming her. Yesenda gazed at Iain with a look of wonder as she matched his pace.

"Oh Iain, you feel so good. Is this how it always is?"

"Only with you," he rasped.

No matter how hard he tried, he could not control his pleasure. He was discovering his wife was a dab hand at love making. Her sheath gripped his length so hard and with such enthusiasm, it was hard to resist. Within minutes, they abandoned all finesse as he rode her hard, pounding inside her over and over.

His hands pressed down on her knees, keeping her spread wide before him as he thrust deep inside repeatedly. He gave a seductive smile when his little spit fire lifted her hips to meet each thrust. Iain wondered how he got so lucky.

Their first time together turned into a frenzied coupling, and Yesenda screamed when she came. Iain swallowed her screams with a kiss. When he felt her core contract around him, he flung his head back and groaned as he exploded inside her.

When they finally came down from the ecstasy they'd just shared, Iain pulled Yesenda into his arms as he murmured sweet nothings in her ear.

He realized he had never had it this good. *Never.*

When they drifted off to sleep, Iain felt as if he finally got his reward. Yesenda was not the 'better' he deserved. She was the *best.*

Hours later, after they had washed and donned bed clothes, Iain asked his wife why she shed her wedding gown without him. Yesenda explained she did not want to rip her fine garments because someday she would pass it onto their daughter. Iain's heart warmed at the sentiment. Yesenda saw a future with him. Even now, their joining could have conceived a child.

As he held her, he splayed one hand protectively across her belly, hoping she would soon cradle their babe inside.

TWO WEEKS PASSED WITHOUT incident, and all was quiet. It seemed the men who had been after Yesenda were no more. The households fell into a comfortable routine, all the while keeping a vigilant eye on the township.

As for the newlywed couple, they could not keep their hands off each other. As they remained in their secluded little world, they hoped that this peace would last forever. But nothing ever does. In hindsight, Iain wished he had savored those moments with Yesenda because days later his entire world would be ripped apart and he would realize this was just the calm before the storm.

Fire!

IT WAS LATE AT NIGHT, and Iain was startled awake.

"Iain! Fire! Wake up," Yesenda shouted as she hastily dressed and grabbed her mace.

He shot straight up, still in a sleep haze.

"Iain, the other cottage is on fire. I'm going to help."

"Wait!" he yelled, but it was too late. Yesenda was already running down the path.

Iain shook himself awake and donned his trews and shoes. He grabbed his sword and ran after Yesenda.

The stable was on fire, and he could hear the horses whinnying inside. He sprinted there first and opened the doors to let them out. Then he veered towards the other cottage.

Yesenda banged on the doors and shutters, trying to wake the occupants. Eventually, Gideon and Sienna emerged with Edmund.

Iain had a weird feeling that something was off. "Gideon, what happened?" he asked as they hauled buckets from the well.

"I dinnae ken. There's no reason for the fire. All the candles were out."

Iain's warning instinct grew stronger, and he never ignored the gut instinct. He said, "Gideon, get Edmund and Sienna out of here. Let the cottage burn."

"Aye, I agree."

They dropped the buckets, and Gideon ran towards Edmund and Sienna. He dragged them away and placed them on the horses.

Iain ran for Yesenda and pulled her with him towards their horse.

"Go to the next location. We will find you," Yesenda said.

Gideon did not hesitate as he clicked his heels, and they rode off into the night.

No sooner had they disappeared when four monks emerged from the bay behind the cottage. They must have sailed in under the cover of darkness.

Yesenda and Iain turned just in time to prepare as the monks came at them. They stood back-to-back. Iain could hear Yesenda's mace clashing with weapons behind him and he blocked and parried blow after blow of war clubs. He noticed, though, no matter how hard they fought; the monks did not seem to want to hurt him. Instead, more just came at Iain until somehow in the melee he got separated from Yesenda.

Then he felt it before he saw it. Something shifted. A monk threw a handful of some substance at Yesenda, and she staggered and swayed.

Iain fought hard to reach her when a dust like substance hit him in the face. He inhaled, and the world became fuzzy.

"Yesenda!" he roared as she turned toward him. She was surrounded. Her face flushed, her eyes drooping. She was mouthing words to him, and just before Iain blacked out, he realized she was saying, "I love you."

St Brendan's Monastery, Clonfert, Ireland

Captive

BISHOP EARL ODO OF Bayeux occupied a seat in his opulent chambers at St Brendan's. They spared no expense in the monastery's building with its Romanesque design, stone edifice, and central sandstone doorways. Celtic designs of carved heads continued to keep watch over the inhabits as they went about their daily lives.

Odo wore his long luxurious designed robe with encrusted jewels sewn into the seams. Underneath, he wore a knee-length embroidered tunic over a pair of hose. He sported a tattoo on the left side of his shoulder. It was an emblem of his order. It displayed a war club crossed over a mace. These were his personal weapons of choice. As a man of the cloth, he could not partake in activities that caused excessive bloodshed. Odo reasoned that caving a man's head in with a club produced minimal bloodshed and, therefore, it was allowed.

He patiently waited for news whilst picking at a platter of fruit when a monk entered the chambers.

"Your Grace, we have found her."

"Well then, bring her to me."

"We chained her up in the prisons below ground."

A flash of irritation crossed Odo's features. He took a deep breath and said, "Then I suggest you release her and give her more comfortable quarters."

"But Your Grace, we thought—"

"Do not argue with me Silas, I will not ask again."

The monk bowed and went to do his bishop's bidding.

Yesenda was dragged out of the prison cell she occupied, still with chains around her wrists. She was still groggy. She hoped Iain was alive, but she doubted he survived the attack. Before she passed out, she saw him collapse onto the ground and her heart broke. Yesenda clenched her fists and willed herself not to think about it or she was likely to burst into tears with a grief that threatened to consume her.

"Where are you taking me? Where am I?" she asked moments later. But the monk ignored her.

He took her to a large, richly decorated chamber. A warm bath and a platter of food and wine awaited her.

"Once you are presentable, the bishop will see you," the monk said.

She was starving, but she dared not eat anything.

The bath looked so inviting; Yesenda felt gritty and clammy. She decided she would have a quick wash and then await her fate.

Moving about the bath shackled with iron was difficult, but she could wash away the dirt and grime. There was a long tunic and feminine robe set out for her, so she donned them as best she could. When she was ready, she was escorted by guards down a long hallway and then seated inside another large chamber. It was there she waited.

The warmth of the fire lulled her to sleep just as the doors opened.

She shook her head and sat upright, and her mouth dropped when she viewed the man walking towards her.

He stretched out his arms and said, "Miriam Ferguson, finally we meet. I am Bishop Odo, glad to make your acquaintance."

Bishop? Yesenda thought if there was any man who could cause a woman to sin, it was him. She was unprepared for such a man. He was young, but there was something otherworldly about him. His dark, seductive eyes reflected every form of vice one could imagine. It was extremely disconcerting the look he gave her. It bored right into her soul and whilst it caused her to shiver, she willed herself to remain calm.

Then she saw it. A spark of interest. A slight softening of his eyes and a leisurely perusal of her body. His eyes rested on her bloodied wrists, the iron shackles, and her swollen split lip, and his face instantly changed and burned with fury. Yesenda flinched and braced herself in the event he would take it out on her.

"Why is she bleeding?" he yelled at a monk hovering a few feet away.

"She did not come quietly, and it took two of us to capture her."

The monk did not see the hit coming. It was so fast. The bishop turned and punched him in the lip until it bled. Then his face was serene when he said, release her bindings and bring water and a bowl of vinegar.

"Bishop, it would not be wise. She could attack—"

"Do as I say, or the next cut you receive will be fatal," he ordered.

The monk rushed away to do the bishop earl's bidding whilst keeping a wide berth.

When they were alone, Odo offered the water vinegar and bowl. He sat beside Yesenda and raised his hand with the cloth to bring it to her face.

"You do not mind, do you?" he asked.

It was incredulous to Yesenda that he would ask, but she shook her head. "'Tis fine," she said.

Odo smiled then. It was so devastating Yesenda wondered if he was Lucifer the fallen angel.

The bishop administered to her wounds with a gentle hand. She grimaced with the sting from the vinegar, and he moved closer. "I am sorry. But the pain was necessary."

She stared into his eyes, and something was happening between them she could not quite understand and, while not uncomfortable, she still did not welcome it.

"You truly are lovely, Miriam. Or should I call you Yesenda?"

She stared up at him in surprise.

He grinned. "Oh, *mademoiselle* you did not think I haven't found out everything about you?"

She shrugged her shoulders.

"Tell me where the boy is."

"What boy?" she feigned ignorance.

"You would truly risk death to protect a useless child?"

"No, I would risk death to keep a vow," she said.

He paused for a while, then reclined again and smiled. "You truly are a breath of fresh air, Miriam Ferguson. Brother Mateo has had a hand in your training, but I would think the softer sentiments can only be from Abbess Murdina. Which is hardly surprising that she would take an interest in her baby brother."

Yesenda looked up in confusion.

"Ah I see you do not know all secrets. Your doting abbess is William's half-sister. She more than anyone knows how ruthless William can be when he feels threatened. Never threaten William with taking his precious dukedom. He has a terrible temper." Odo shuddered.

Yesenda still held a confused expression.

Odo sighed and said, "The duke and I are half-brothers through our mother. Your abbess and the duke are half siblings through their father, Robert. Her real name is 'Adeliza' but as you go by the name Miriam, she uses Murdina and little Edmund, who you protect so viciously, is—"

"Her baby brother," Yesenda said. Suddenly, it made so much sense. Abbess Murdina did everything in her power to protect the babe.

"No matter what you think of me, I do not kill babies. Besides, our religious ways do not condone infanticide or violence."

"And yet you wield the war club," Yesenda said.

"And you wield the mace," he replied. "For the church to survive, sometimes we must take up arms and protect ourselves."

"I still will not tell you anything. I have only your word and unless I can confirm the truth of the matter, my position does not change."

"Rightly so. But you know I only have everyone's best interests at heart."

"How so?" Yesenda asked.

"Well, I am perfectly happy with William remaining the duke. I have many luxuries afforded to me because he is a duke and a doting brother. However, I am also respectful of the power and influence his sister wields among the religious orders. So, it's in my best interest to appease both sides."

"Why are you so eager to find Edmund?"

"So, I can protect him from William but also keep him in a comfortable lifestyle, so he feels no need to challenge the dukedom. That way William remains duke and I keep Adeliza happy."

Yesenda scrunched her face up at him.

"My dear, I am not the big bad ogre everyone makes me out to be. I am just a simple man trying to make his way in the world."

Yesenda remained skeptical.

"Well, my dear, it has been truly enlightening speaking to you. Leave everything to me. I see no reason to detain you any further."

"But you've been trying to kill me all this time. Why would you set me free now? Is this trickery?"

He looked genuinely shocked at her statement.

"Oh, my dear, I have done no such thing. I sent my brethren to *Glencoe* but not to do harm."

"Yet one of them tried to kill the laird's wife and bairn. He was specifically searching for a Miriam Ferguson."

"Believe me, if I wanted you dead, you would be dead. The only reason you're alive is because I warned my men not to harm you. To date, none have been killed. So, whoever they have sent to kill you, are certainly not my men."

"Then who are they? They say they work for the bishop and for England."

Odo paced slightly, then he paused and asked, "Is there anyone else in your little town who is usually not from there?"

"How do you mean?"

"Well, people who work for nobles usually come and go. They rarely stay long in one place; however, they will revisit when it is convenient."

It finally dawned on Yesenda. *Liosa.*

The bishop called Silas over.

"Your Grace?"

"Send a missive and call off the search."

"But the duke—"

"The duke does not need to know a damn thing."

Silas nodded.

Then Odo said, "Yesenda, it is possible whoever wants you dead may be driven by reasons other than what you think."

The Angel

YESENDA WAS MOVED TO a chamber on the lower floor and arrangements were being made for her safe passage home. Odo refused to let her travel alone, so she was forced to wait a couple of days before they arranged an escort. In the meantime, she fretted and worried over Iain. The bishop insisted his men did not kill the burly Highlander. Yesenda would not believe it until she saw Iain face to face. She could only guess Iain would be worried sick about her.

That night, she was having a fitful sleep when an Angel of the lord appeared before her. He was a demigod with long blond hair and deep blue eyes. His features were chiseled. Yesenda had to marvel at such beauty and perfection.

Then he said in a strange accent, "Yesenda, hold on, lass. I'll get you out of here."

"Am I dead? Are you an angel?" she whispered.

He chuckled quietly, "No, my name is Torstein, and Sorcha sent me. My *snekkja* awaits."

He carried her out of the chamber and down to a longboat waiting on the shores of the monastery.

Yesenda woke several times to the feel of the floor rocking beneath her and she heard the sea.

Then she saw a beloved face hovering above her.

"Iain?"

"Aye, love. Stay with me. You have a fever."

"I love you, Iain."

"I love you too, sweeting."

"Are you taking me home?"

"Aye, we're going home."

Sometime later she woke again, still feverish, and she saw the beautiful angel.

"Hello angel from heaven," she said.

Torstein started chortling. "You better not call me that lass or that big brute beside you will try to punch me again."

She saw it was Iain and said, "Oh, he's not a brute. He is my husband."

"Such a pity, the pretty ones are always taken," Torstein said with a wink.

Chapter 17

Henderson Land, Glencoe

Three weeks later, all was well again. Iain and Yesenda were back on Henderson land. Gideon, Sienna and Edmund were settled in a safe place, and Brother Mateo had since joined them. Bishop Odo was true to his word, and the threat to Edmund had passed. They spread word far and wide that the family who lived in the cottage at *Kentallen* had all perished, including a young lad by the name of Edmund.

It was still unclear why Yesenda was being targeted since no one had seen Liosa for a while.

But the truth always comes out. When it did, they realized they should have been paying better attention.

The Attack

YESENDA WALKED TO THE training grounds at the Keep. Since their return, Bram had asked her if she would like to train some warriors. She knew she could teach them a lot. Yesenda wore trews, tunic, and long cloak. Her mace was strapped to her side. Iain had retrieved it from *Kentallen*. She was lost in thought when she spied a familiar person walking ahead. It was Silas, the monk who worked for Bishop Odo. She frowned in confusion, wondering why he was there.

Suddenly, Silas turned abruptly and said, "Finally, I get to kill you properly."

Yesenda paused and said, "So Bishop Odo lied. He is the one who wants me dead?"

Silas laughed. "No, Matilda of Flanders, the duke's wife, pays me handsomely to spy on Odo. She does not trust him at all. I am here because she does not want anyone taking the dukedom from William."

Things seemed to click into place for Yesenda. She remembered the missive at Gibson farm. The 'M' seal addressed to 'Brother S' and it all made sense now.

"What are you going to do, monk?" Yesenda asked, preparing herself for the attack.

"My job is to kill anyone who can prove Edmund is the legitimate heir. That includes you," Silas said.

"Well, you can certainly try," Yesenda replied.

She sensed someone behind her and turned to see Liosa stepping out of the bushes.

"What are you doing here, Liosa?" she asked, taking a step back from both.

"I am making sure my patroness Matilda gets what she wants," Liosa replied. "I have been her informant for many years. From the moment you arrived, you ruined everything for me."

Iain was heading to the Keep when he noticed something strange ahead. He crept quietly in the shadows, listening to the conversation whilst inching his way closer to Yesenda. He sensed she was in grave danger. Iain heard everything and could not believe the treachery of Liosa. All this time Liosa worked for *Matilda of Flanders*, and now she thought to kill Yesenda.

Yesenda pulled out her mace and was bracing herself to take them both on.

She was so busy monitoring them both she failed to see the mini cross bow until it was too late. Silas raised his arm. It was concealed inside the sleeve of his robe. He shot two arrows at close range. Yesenda tried to dodge them, but one hit her chest and the other lodged deep into her side.

"No!" Iain roared as he came running down the pathway with his claymore.

Silas turned and aimed at Iain, but Yesenda moved faster. Blood was pouring from her side, but she raised her mace high and brought it crashing down on Silas's arm, diverting the direction of the arrow. Silas's arrow went wide and pierced Liosa's skull. Liosa's shocked expression was frozen on her face when she fell down dead.

Iain brought his claymore down, skewering Silas's chest.

The threat removed, Yesenda finally calmed, realizing blood was dripping down her chest and her side. Her whole body felt wet. She looked down to see blood oozing onto the handle of her mace. It slipped out of her fingers. She staggered backward and felt the world spinning. She saw Iain running towards her, shouting her name. All she heard was a loud buzzing sound. Iain caught her body before she hit the ground.

"No! No! Dinnae leave me!" Iain yelled.

Yesenda attempted to lift her hand to caress his face, but she was too weak and finally she slipped into oblivion.

Iain roared in anguish as he held Yesenda tight. He lifted her into his arms and felt her blood seeping into his clothes. Then he ran for the Keep.

Iain burst into the Great Hall of the Keep, his wife unconscious in his arms.

He roared, "Tyra! Sorcha! Help me, please, somebody help me." His words were indecipherable as he rocked Yesenda in his arms saying, "Stay with me, love, please dinnae leave me."

Iain heard people running toward him. But all he focused on was Yesenda's face, drained of life. He was sobbing when Tyra and Sorcha appeared with worry etched on their faces. They began shouting orders to people in the distance.

"Cousin, we need to put her on the table." Iain looked up to see Bram in front of him, reaching for Yesenda. He saw Niall and Lachlan running and fetching things for Tyra and Sorcha. He saw his aunt Fia and cousin Willa throwing sheets on the table, issuing orders to serving women.

Iain realized he was not alone. He had family and his clan. Yesenda had a chance. "Aye," he said as Bram helped him get Yesenda to the table.

Ten Days Later

"IAIN?" YESENDA RASPED.

"Aye love I am here."

"Are you well, Iain? She reached up and cupped his cheek."

Iain kissed the inside of her palm and said, "I am."

She grinned, then her eyes fluttered again, and she was out cold.

"Yesenda!" He grabbed her limp hand, half panicking.

"'Tis alright Iain, she will be alright, come let us tend to her," Sorcha said.

"She just needs her rest, Iain," Willa added.

He nodded; his heart filled to overflowing. They almost lost Yesenda twice in the first week. Fortunately, his wife was a fighter, and she was now recovering well. The danger had passed, and Iain was relieved.

But now he was assailed with guilt. Guilt because his ex-lover hurt the woman he loved. Iain was ashamed that Yesenda paid the price for his weakness and failure in letting Liosa enter their lives. He rued the day Yesenda despised him for the pain she had suffered.

Guilty Feet

IT WAS THE THIRD WEEK of Yesenda's recovery and Iain was out at the tavern getting blind drunk.

"Leave me alone," he said to Kieran.

"Why aren't you by your wife's bedside?"

"She's lying in that bed because of me. My life choices almost got her killed. I cannot bear to see the blame in her eyes. Liosa was plotting to kill her, and I did nothing about it."

"Because you did not ken it. But right now, you have a bonnie wife calling for you and you're failing her by making one poor decision after another."

"But I have failed her already."

"Och horse shit! You stupid prick. You've got your head so far up your arse you cannot see she needs you more than ever now."

"She does not need me. I will only drag her down."

"For fuck's sake! Stop ya blathering," Kieran growled. "If you dinnae see her soon, you're going to lose her forever because she will think you dinnae love her anymore."

Iain's head shot up. "But I love her more than my own life."

"Well, you're acting like a man who doesna ken what love is. To be honest, I think it'll serve you right if she leaves your worthless *bahookie* and marries someone else. Perhaps that pretty Norseman. What's his name again? Torstein. That's him. They will make bonnie bairns together—"

"Get out of my way!" Iain shouted as he stood up and pushed Kieran aside. "Over my dead body will she be making bairns with that pretty, angel faced maggot!"

Iain raced outside.

"Iain!" Kieran yelled.

"Dinnae stop me. I am going to see my wife."

"Aye. But you're going the wrong way. The Keep is that way." Kieran pointed in the opposite direction.

Iain looked around and realized he was correct. He changed course and said, "I ken it."

Kieran just shook his head and muttered, "Just dinnae end up in Rome."

Henderson Keep

THERE WAS A KNOCK AT the door. Yesenda sat up and in walked Iain with some wildflowers. She drank in the sight of him, but then lowered her head, seeing that he had a resigned expression on his face.

He paused for the longest time, just gazing at her. His heartbeat faster and all he could see was her.

"Can I speak to you, love?"

She shrugged her shoulders. She knew what was coming. Iain was going to tell her he was leaving and that he blamed her for Liosa's death. Yesenda braced for the news and took deep calming breaths and then stared out the window. She could hear the shuffling of feet as he pulled up a chair closer to the bed.

Iain placed the flowers on the bed. He cleared his throat, and for a moment, he was just stunned. He could not stop gazing at his wife. She was the loveliest woman he'd ever seen. In that moment, his doubts melted away.

"Yesenda. Please look at me."

She turned her head, and he saw a sheen of moisture glistening in her eyes. Iain mentally kicked his own ass for causing her distress.

When a solitary tear slid down her cheek, Ian reached out and wiped it with his thumb, then whispered, "Please dinnae cry *mo leannan*. I am sorry. I am so sorry."

Yesenda braced, waiting for him to deliver the blow.

"What are you sorry about, Iain?" she asked.

"I am sorry that I did not visit you earlier. I am sorry for so many things. I'm sorry that it's taken me so long to tell you."

"Just say it, Iain, and do it quickly. You're exasperating," Yesenda snapped.

"All right, calm down, woman."

Then Yesenda saw red. "Calm down? You want me to calm down?"

"Aye, you're getting yourself worked up for no reason."

"No reason? No reason?" she screeched.

"Yesenda! Why are you yelling at me like a banshee? I've come here to tell you something very important."

Her patience done, her composure went out the window when Yesenda shouted, "I'm yelling at you because you're a bloody idiot! That's why. You're a stupid fool who cannot ken his head from his ass."

Iain paused and blinked at her in confusion as she carried on.

"And despite all that, I still love you! But do you care? Not one bit. I've been lying in this bloody bed for days and you abandoned me. Discarded me like a rotten piece of cabbage. Oh but now that I'm well, you come in here just to tell me you're leaving me because I got Liosa killed?"

So caught up in her tirade, she failed to notice his entire body lock, and his eyes softened.

"Love, I dinnae blame you—"

Yesenda continued, "Well, guess what, Iain Henderson, you can rot in hell and take your stupid flowers with you!" She picked them up off the bed and threw them at him, then folded her arms and glared.

Iain rose from his chair and sat down beside her on the bed. Nudging her so he could fit on the edge.

"Get off my bed. You're taking up all the room."

She continued to glare at him. When he said, "Have you finished, love? Can I speak now?"

"Do what you want Iain, I dinnae care anymore." She sniffed.

"You still love me?" he asked.

Her face went red, and she hissed, "Out of everything I just said, that's all you heard?"

Before she could continue, Iain cupped her face and kissed her soundly on the lips. Yesenda stiffened, but he was persistently seeking entry with his tongue. She sighed and returned the kiss for all it was worth. Yesenda figured if this was the last time she was going to see this man, she would steal enough to last a lifetime.

Iain whispered across her lips, "I came here to tell you I love you, and I am sorry it was my fault they attacked you. I dinnae blame you for anything. I am just sorry I stayed away and caused you even more pain."

"Wait, so you're not leaving me?"

"Never. If you had let me speak instead of screeching at me, I would have explained it already."

"I dinnae screech."

"Let's not ruin this moment arguing about your bellowing."

She glared at him, then just shook her head.

"Iain gently picked her up and placed her on his lap, then he kissed her some more."

Iain's Cottage, Henderson Land

"IAIN! OOH, RIGHT THERE. Just. Like. That!" Yesenda shouted in pleasure.

She was on her hands and knees while Iain was pounding her from behind. His large hands gripped her breasts for purchase as he plunged his engorged length in and out of her.

"Argh!" he groaned as he thrust into her harder and faster." His breathing was erratic as perspiration dripped from his chest.

"Aye, that's it," Yesenda rasped. Her hair was plastered to her face from perspiration. They had been enjoying a bout of rigorous love making for over an hour and still neither one would concede defeat.

"You feel so good, love," Iain groaned as Yesenda contracted her core tighter around him.

He moved his arm to her belly and flipped her onto the bed as he continued to thrust inside. One hand sought her clit, and he rigorously massaged her while his other hand pinched her taut nipple.

"Ooh, Iain," she moaned, as his thumb pressed down harder. Yesenda moaned, then her eyes rolled to the back of her head as she came. Iain groaned and thrust several times before he burst and filled her with his seed.

Iain continued to caress her as his hips kept flicking upward. Yesenda rode the edge of her orgasm with her hips, milking him dry.

Eventually, their movements slowed, and their ragged breathing evened out.

Iain captured her lips with his own. Then he whispered, "I love you."

"Not as much as I love you," she replied.

As they lay together in sated bliss, they heard a loud banging on the door and shouting.

They were both up in an instant. Yesenda barely got her chemise on, and Iain threw his paid around his middle before the door burst open to reveal Ruadh MacDonald in the doorway.

He looked from Iain to Yesenda, and their state of undress, and he lost his ever-loving mind. Ruadh lunged at Iain and planted a fist in his face.

Yesenda grabbed her mace and blocked Ruadh from hitting Iain again. "Dinnae touch my husband, Ruadh!"

"For goodness' sake, wife," Iain muttered and tried to pull Yesenda behind him.

Ruadh paused and looked at them.

"What did you just call my sister?" Ruadh asked Iain. His voice was laced with steel.

"We're married, and it's consummated," Yesenda said.

Ruadh roared, then launched himself at Iain with his fist flying. He landed one punch in which Iain did not defend himself against. He was going for another when Yesenda moved so fast to block it with her forearm. Then she grabbed his fist in one hand and, in a maneuver Ruadh had not expected, yanked his arm around his back so Ruadh's face was shoved up against the wall.

"I told you not to touch my husband," she growled.

"Ouch, bloody hell sister, what are you doing?" Ruadh gasped through restricted lungs.

Yesenda saw Ruadh's guardsman entering the fray from the side of her eye. She kicked the handle of her mace into the air and caught it with her free hand and pointed it at him. "Dinnae even think about it. This is between me and my brother," she hissed.

The guardsman raised his hands in surrender and took a step back.

Iain just smiled and said, "Wise choice, warrior."

"All right. Gods' teeth, let go!" Ruadh shook her off him. "You're lucky I dinnae hit women, or you'd be—"

"She'd be just fine, Ruadh. Tis you who would be flat on your arse," Iain said.

Yesenda grinned at Iain and winked.

Ruadh said, "For crying out loud, someone better explain what is happening before I cast up my accounts. You sicken me. Both of you."

"Your sister and I were married by a priest two months ago. We didna have time to inform you, but there was a letter from Bram. Do you object to the marriage?" Iain asked.

Ruadh sighed and said, "No, but put some bloody clothes on, both of you. I dinnae want to think about what you've been doing in here." He shuddered and walked out, slamming the door behind him.

Epilogue

1049 Healer's Cottage, Henderson Land

Iain was aimlessly running and shouting, "The bairn is coming! The bairn is coming! Dinnae fash, you need to remain calm, stay calm."

"*Wheesht*, Iain. Will you stop moving about?" Yesenda hissed. She was on the bed, trying to focus on her breathing as another contraction hit.

"Tyra is coming, but she gave me these herbs to prepare. It should help soothe you till our babe arrives. I need to mix it in hot water." Iain held up the small pouch, then ran about the cottage, panicking. He grabbed the water jug and poured water into a cup, then yelled, "This bloody water is cold! How do I make hot water?"

Yesenda just rolled her eyes.

"Move," Torstein said. He nudged Iain out of the way, poured water into a pot, then set it over the fire.

Iain paused, realizing for the first time that Torstein was in the cottage. "What are you bloody doing in here with my wife?"

"I carried her inside because you almost passed out," Torstein replied.

"Hey, dinnae look at my wife down there." Iain glared at Torstein.

"I am not looking down there. I am trying to help, not ravish her."

"I dinnae care. Close your eyes." Iain placed his hands over Torstein's eyes.

"I cannot see anything, you idiot." Torstein slapped Iain's hands away.

"That's the point. I ken what you Norsemen are about, trying to steal our women from us."

"You really have no sense, do you? If I can steal your woman while she is birthing your bairn, then that says more about your wooing skills."

"My woman would not be about to push out my bairn if I didna have great wooing skills," Iain growled.

"Your woman will not be your woman much longer if you keep arguing while I bring your stubborn son into the world." Yesenda bit her lip when she felt a sharp pain.

Iain paled and said, "My daughter is not stubborn. She is just strong willed like her *màthair*."

"Iain, I think the babe is coming soon," Yesenda rasped.

"Leave now Tor, only I get to see my woman's parts, not you."

Torstein glared at Iain. "Do you honestly think I want to be here? There are many women I can tup who are far less trouble than this one. No offence Yesenda."

"Tis all right. Now can someone please help me deliver this bairn? because I feel like my insides are being torn apart."

At those words, Iain stopped breathing, and fainted near the fireplace.

Yesenda just shook her head. Moments later, the door opened, and Tyra arrived.

"Oh, thank the lord, Tyra, please get these two out of here," Yesenda pleaded.

"I am so sorry I got here as fast as I could. But where is Iain? I gave him a brew for you to drink."

"He's over there," Torstein said, gesturing towards the fireplace.

Tyra just shook her head and said, "Men. Bloody useless. They easily get a bairn inside a woman then faint at the sight of one coming out."

"The water is hot, so I'll take my leave," Torstein said as he hauled Iain up and sat him on a chair.

"CONGRATULATIONS BROTHER, you have a healthy baby son. Now let's hope he takes after his *màthair* and not his da," Tyra said.

Iain nursed his head wound and crawled his way over to the bed, where Yesenda cradled their newborn. The reverence with which he gazed at his family was something to behold.

"He's ours?" he whispered.

"Aye Iain, he's ours."

Iain's eyes glistened with unshed tears as he caressed the babe's cheek. He then gently leaned forward and brushed a kiss across Yesenda's lips.

"Thank you for giving me a son," he said.

"Dinnae be silly. It took the two of us, Iain."

"Aye, I ken it. I was there, wife. Every single time, loving every moment."

Yesenda just smiled with love shining through.

Iain's mood became somber when he said, "Yesenda, after the pain I saw you go through, there'll be no more planting bairns in your belly."

Yesenda raised a brow. "Is that so?"

"Aye, tis so. You'll not be having your seductive way with me anymore, wife."

"Our son needs siblings, Iain, or he will get bored."

We could think about it in five years. I cannot go through this again."

She raised her eyebrow. "*You* cannot go through this again? Iain Henderson, just you try to stay away from me. I am very determined."

Iain grinned. "Then I have no chance."

"None whatsoever."

Sorcha's Solar, Henderson Keep – *14 Weeks Later*

"SORCHA, HE IS SO FRUSTRATING. He will not come near me. Do you think Iain no longer finds me attractive?" Yesenda asked.

"Yesenda, you could be fat, thin, bald, have scales on your back, and warts on your nose, and that man would still desire you."

"How can I get him to be intimate with me again?"

"I am sure Iain is suffering as much as you and, after many weeks of abstinence, he would be fit to burst. What you need to do is trap him and seduce him."

"How?"

Sorcha grinned. "I forget sometimes that you grew up in an abbey. But the answer is simple. All you need to do is talk to Iain and clarify that you desire him, and you need him to give you pleasure."

"I've tried that already."

"Ah... but did you have the talk with him while you were *naked?*"

Yesenda raised her eyebrow. "Ah... no."

"Trust me, do it without your clothes on. Tis far more effective if you want to get your own way."

"And this really works?"

Sorcha said, "When Cináed was born, it was a terrible ordeal for Bram to witness. The same thing happened."

"What did you do?"

"I had to seduce my husband and make him understand this was just the way of things. If a bairn resulted, then so be it."

"I guess it worked, seeing as you're expecting again."

"Aye, it did. A good man will always be afraid for his woman. All we can do is keep loving them through the fear."

"You truly are wise Sorcha Henderson. I am so glad you married Bram. He is lucky to have you."

"Oh, I am not wise. I grew up in MacGregor Keep. Stubborn men have surrounded me my whole life and then I married one. One thing I have learned is when they love it is deep and sometimes you need to help them trust everything will be all right."

Yesenda nodded, taking in all this newfound wisdom.

Then Sorcha added, "But it still helps to be naked while doing it."

They burst out laughing.

Iain's Cottage, Henderson Land – Life is Life

"IAIN, COME HERE, PLEASE. Can you pass me that plaid? I just need to put something warm around me." Yesenda stepped out of her bath completely nude, her body glistening from the water, and Iain went rock hard in an instant. He held his breath as he watched her move towards the fire and dry herself. She had filled out some after the birth of their babe. The midwife said it was safe to resume relations again, but Iain would not risk it. He knew his wife was using her wiles on him.

Yesenda tied up her hair in front of the fire. Her breasts were full, and her figure was shapelier. She carried weight around her middle with a slight bump to show where she had cradled his bairn inside her. Iain inhaled a sharp breath, his mouth wide open, trying not to lust after his wife, but it was no use. He longed to run his tongue across every inch of her.

Yesenda patted the towel across her body, and, like a siren's song, she beckoned to him.

"Iain? Are you going to stand there gawking all night? Or are you going to come and help me get ready for bed?" She gave him a coy glance, giving him a view of her shapely thighs and backside.

"What?" Iain rasped and swallowed hard.

"Come and join me by the fire. So, you can keep me warm." She turned to face him, and Iain just groaned.

"See something you like, Iain?"

"Damn you woman, put some bloody clothes on now," he growled as he threw a plaid at her.

"Oh, I appear to be very clumsy of late," Yesenda said, deliberately dropping the plaid.

"Dinnae give me that. You can catch a mace and a bloody arrow. Are you trying to make me lose my resolve?" He clenched his fists, so he did not reach out for her.

Yesenda went in for the kill. "Aye, husband I am. I have a frightful need to be pleasured. I need to feel your mouth suckling me here." She caressed her breasts. "And I need your hard shaft deep inside me here." She moved her hand down between her thigh to caress her heat. "And I need your tongue—"

Yesenda gave a high-pitched yelp because before she could finish her sentence, Iain was across the room hoisting her over his shoulder. He strode towards the bed and tossed her on it as he began undoing his trews.

"Damn you and your seductive ways."

She giggled.

Then Iain paused and said with concern, "Are you sure, love? I cannot bear to see you suffer any pain. If anything happens to you, I will not survive it."

She caressed his jaw and said, "Iain, life is life. We must live it the best we can and be thankful for each day."

"My wife is a wise woman."

"Aye, I am. No matter what happens, dinnae deny me the honor of loving you."

He smiled then and whispered, "All right, you've convinced me."

Yesenda chuckled as Iain's mouth and body covered hers. Soon her mirth turned into moans. Then the pent-up passion from weeks of abstinence turned into an insatiable, primal need. There was no gentleness or finesse. It was purely physical. Two people long denied battling for supremacy between the sheets.

"You're so bonnie, my love. Especially when you're riding me so hard," Iain groaned as he thrust inside his wife.

Yesenda was riding astride. Her palms were flat on Iain's chest, digging into his skin, using his chest for balance. Her head was thrown back with her glorious locks spilling across her shoulders. Iain gloried at the sight of her ample breasts bouncing above his head. He leant forward and suckled the stiffened peaks. She was still nursing. The taste of her exploded on his tongue. Each time he did it, he felt her contract around him and he clenched his jaw with the sensation.

Iain's hands gripped her hips and dug into her flesh as he coaxed her body to move in rhythm with his thrusts. Yesenda's hips were jerking so fast Iain could barely hold on. Her channel gripped him tight and deep as she rode with abandon. She impaled herself on his full length, then released all the way to the tip, then plunged down repeatedly. Iain took his fill as he matched her thrusts. He bottomed out and heard her moaning with pleasure. It was music to his ears.

"Love, I cannot hold much longer. You need to finish," he growled.

"No, I want more."

"Greedy wench," he said as he slapped her backside.

"Give me more, husband!" she shouted.

Iain threw his head back, trying not to come before her, but he was fast losing the battle.

His hand shot out to where they joined, and he vigorously rubbed her heated pearl.

"Come, now," he demanded.

"You're cheating," Yesenda gasped, then her entire body stiffened. Her walls contracted so hard around his length as she came.

"Damn!" Iain roared as he thrust three more times and climaxed with satisfaction.

Later, Yesenda was sprawled on top of him. Her head tucked into the crook of his shoulder as she gasped for air.

Iain was trying to catch his breath. One arm was draped across her back, holding her close and running his fingers through her hair. "Gads, woman, you almost killed me," he said.

Yesenda lifted her head, seeking his lips as he lowered his mouth and kissed her.

They were lying in the afterglow of another sensational joining, the third that night, and their faces were inches apart. Not saying anything, just enjoying being in each other's presence. Yesenda's hands continued to caress Iain's chest and arms.

They needed no words between them. Their eyes expressed the love they felt.

Life is life. Iain thought as he treasured these moments with the love of his life.

He was just drifting off to sleep when baby Oban let out a wail from the adjoining room. Iain shot straight up and was out of bed donning his plaid. He bent and kissed Yesenda on the tip of her nose, then hurried to fetch his son.

Yesenda lay back, propped on her elbows as she watched Iain cradle their babe in his arms while cooing softly.

Life is life. She thought. At that moment, Yesenda knew hers was perfect.

Three Months Later

IAIN STRODE INTO THEIR cottage and said, "Guess what, love?"

Yesenda looked up from polishing her mace. "What?"

"Bram received a missive from Kieran."

"And?"

"Kieran is wed."

She paused, then asked, "To whom?"

"Naomi!" Iain declared as if it were the juiciest gossip in the world.

"What? When?" Yesenda asked.

"I dinnae ken the details. But I never would have put those two together."

Yesenda put aside the mace and said, "But Naomi hates him."

Iain sat down beside her and said, "Aye, and Kieran dislikes her with equal measure. Bram said there are matters they must deal with first before they return."

"What matters?"

"Something to do with Torstein."

"Well, I just hope they're safe," she said.

Iain replied, "If Naomi is anything like you, I very much doubt it."

The End

Kieran and Naomi's Story - Coming Soon.
https://elinaemerald.com/books

Series & Book Order

Reformed Rogues Series (Medieval Romance)
    Book 1: Betrothed to the Beast (Beiste & Amelia)
Book 2: Handfasted to the Bear (Brodie & Orla)
Book 3: Pledged to the Wolf (Dalziel & Clarissa)
Series continues to spin-offs...
The MacGregors (Medieval Romance)
Book 1: Arrowsmith (Ewan & Beth)
Book 2: Sorcha (Bram & Sorcha)
Book 3: Lachlan (Lachie & Tyra)
Highland Warrior: Keeper of Secrets (Ian & Yesenda)
Highland Guard: Keeper of Secrets II (Kieran & Naomi)

Author Notes

If you'd like to know how I ended up writing this story, head to my website blog and enjoy my rambling notes. https://elinaemerald.com/blog/f/author-notes-for-highland-warrior-keeper-of-secrets

Also by Elina Emerald

Cambridge
Lucas

Fragrance
No Promises
No Games

FRIVEN EMPIRE
The Eleventh House
The Vedora Key

Keeper of Secrets
Highland Warrior: Keeper of Secrets

Reformed Rogues
Betrothed to the Beast
Betrothed to the Beast

Handfasted to the Bear
Pledged to the Wolf

The MacGregors
Arrowsmith
Sorcha
Lachlan

Watch for more at https://elinaemerald.com/books.